482

I,
MORGAIN

by Harry Robin

Branden Publishing Company, Inc.
Boston

Library of Congress Cataloging-in-Publication Data

Robin, Harry.
    I, Morgain : a novella / by Harry Robin
       p. cm.
    ISBN 0-8283-2004-7
    1. Morgan le Fay (Legendary character)--
       Fiction.
    2. Arthurian romances--Adaptations.
    I. Title
    PS3568.026512   1955
    813'.54--dc20   94-42544
                                CIP

BRANDEN PUBLISHING COMPANY, Inc.
17 Station Street
843 Brookline Village
Boston, MA 02147

FOREWORD

This book is the end result of several fortunate accidents. Each time I have been to Paris I've made at least one visit to the bookstalls on the Pont Neuf. A sweet, older woman tended one of them and she remembered me each time I visited. Madame Douvrie knew my rather quirky interests and she would offer a volume, or a page of an illustrated book--"It may interest you, monsieur."

On my last visit Madame Douvrie greeted me with pleasure again. She offered me a small volume with a yellowed, battered, unlettered, heavy cardboard cover. I thanked her and opened the book. It was printed in Welsh, a language I find strange to look at, with its *llechways* and *ymdaneis* and *ffedeirs*. But I could recognize the subject of the book from its title page: *Morgain*. It was about Morgain, the half-sister of King Arthur.

I am familiar with the Arthurian legends and knew about Morgain and her role in them. I bought the book, even though I knew that reading it would be impossible. When I returned home I put it on the shelf that holds my small collection of books in languages other than English. That section of my library assures me that I don't have to read every book I own.

About a year ago I went to England to do research on a new project. An old friend invited me to a dinner party. There I met a man whose first name was the same as my own, who was born in the same month and year as I, and who shared my delight in the iconoclasms we both knew to be absolute values. He is a Welshman with a great passion for the beauties of the Welsh language. He demonstrated that passion by reciting stanzas of old Welsh elegies and curses. They were wonderfully musical, although I could not of course understand a single word.

He expressed an avid interest in the Morgain book. We drew up and signed an agreement after we'd had our desserts and tea: he would make a literal translation of the Morgain book, and I would rewrite, edit, and seek a publisher for it.

What follows is the result of those small wonders.

H.R.

NOTE:

The events recounted in this autobiography may have occurred sometime during the fifth and/or sixth centuries A.D., according to generally accepted Arthurian scholarship. Morgain evidently dictated her reminiscences to her cousin and lady-in-waiting, Lady Ceinwen.

The Welsh people did not have a written language in this period. The Druids's written language was rudimentary, because of their devotion to the oral (bardic) tradition. Lady Ceinwen may have been educated in Latin by an Irish Christian priest, one of several whose mission was to persuade the Britons to adopt the new Christian faith.

We may conjecture that the little book's original Latin was translated much later into Welsh.

Our heroine's name was Morgain, or Morrigan. Those who think it should be written as "Morgain la Faye" are advised to avoid the snares of anachronism, which so often commingle history with fable. "La Faye" ("the enchantress") is the cognomen attached to Morgain in the Arthurian legends that were written at least five or six centuries after she had passed out of this life into the Druid's "Otherworld."

6 -- Harry Robin

Although we can only speculate on the matter of provenance, there can be no question of our admiration of, and our gratitude to Lady Ceinwen. *In memoriam*.

☼

I,
MORGAIN

He is dead. Our king, my brother, is dead. I know that Arthur's passing was written in our stars. But even so, I did not want it, and--by my gods and goddesses!--certainly not in this way. I used every potion I know to try to heal those terrible wounds. Their stench hangs in this chamber still. I must open the curtains, we must cleanse this air. It will help his spirit move onward.

The water is so still. There in the mist, just beginning to escape from the darkening waters, rise the vapor dragons. We have fought them well, many times. No fear now, my lonely heart.

Ceinwen, call the other women. We must prepare my brother for his passage.

☆

Even now, in his passage, his face is so beautiful. The scars of old wounds intensify his manliness. His nose and mouth, so like my mother's. And now his eyes, with their lush gold lashes, are closed. They will never, those blue flames, never pierce my own again.

My ladies' tears are quiet. But they grieve, yes, I know they grieve. My eyes are dry. But I, too, grieve. As we dress his broken body in the great purple robe, I look out to my oak, the venerable one. Its leaves are gone, its branches black strokes in the fading light.

This body will dissolve and become dust. But my brother, Arthur, King Arthur, will remain alive. In memory, he will live forever.

✿

I can summon up images, sounds, faces, the ridges of muscles in terror and pleasure. Does memory die when I die?

But my death, like this one on the dark table, will be only another passage. Quiet, now, quiet, my lonely heart. He will live in memory, Arthur the King--as will I, Morgain.

There!

In the dark boat he lies, ready for the journey to the Land of the Young. Now his quiet face and folded hands are all that can be seen of what was once a man. I have seen that deep, deep quiet in the faces of so many men and women in the moments of their passage.

Acceptance? Confidence in the prospect of the new voyage?

☼

We placed the mistletoe in his stiff fingers. We pushed the long, black boat off the shore. As the boat and its precious passenger glided away on the glassy water, we made our circle holding hands, and we sang:

Now, under the bowl of the purpling sky,
Cradled in the waters,
>You are a king, again.
>You were a gilded spear,
>You held a terrible sword.
>You made the earth shiver,
>You tore the ferns and crushed the
>>heather.
>But in the Land of the Young to
>>which you go,
>You will learn that we are born,
>Grow old, and die.
>Those are the parts,
>That is the sum.

As we watched the boat carry him away we were gladdened by a sign from our gods and goddesses. The sun, dipping below the far rim of the water, splashed the sky with rose, peach, and gold. We bowed our heads as the black boat disappeared in the mists.

☼

Now, as even before his passage, they will tell Arthur's deeds throughout the land. But no man knows what I have experienced and learned. There is so much fawning over the deeds of men, and so contemptible an ignorance of what we women know and do. Or do men know us, but hide from that knowledge?

I have not escaped the vices in myself, my pride, my jealousy, my lasciviousness. But neither have I been ignorant of my virtues, my devotion to my wondermaking gods and goddesses, my loyalty to friends. My ladies, working here now, will speak to that.

Lady Ceinwen, who writes my words as I speak, is an old and tired woman now. Ettarde, brilliant and mad as a rabbit in the springtime. Niniane, so graceful, wise, and ever at the edge of evil. Yet none of them, even as close to me as they are, knows the full, true course of my life. So I shall tell my life in whatever time is left to me before I move to the Otherworld.

☼

When my first blood flowed, in my shift from child to maiden, my mother, Ygraine of Cornwall, told me of my birthing. How, on a fragrant spring morning, as the first rays of the sun shot out over the ocean below, she began her birthing trials. I was her first child, or so she said. She spoke of her delight and expectation that were arrested by the sharp, tearing pains as I began to move out into this world. And she told me that she tried for a whole day until I finally breathed air, late that night.

There was a warm rain, and my nurse bathed me in its sweet falling drops under the night sky. Her name was Laba, and she passed over many winters ago. Laba once told me that far above the rain, she could clearly see the Great Water Carrier in the stars that night.

✧

I believe I remember everything. All, that is, but my first year. My mother was so delighted with me that she often repeated her stories. So I am not always sure that I truly remember what happened in my early childhood--or if I was told what happened. And yet I have never had reason to question the truth of whatever she told me, in her love and delight, each time I was in her presence.

My father, Gorlois, Duke of Cornwall in the Castle of Tintagel, occupied himself with the tasks of a great lord. There were peasants, crafts-men, the stables, the dairy. And armorers and wars, in which men try, even today, to steal the holdings of other men, or try to protect their own from being stolen.

☼

Of all his holdings, Ygraine, my mother, was my father's most precious. He loved her obsessively and was quickly jealous of her attention. I did not--of course, I could not--know this in terms of man and woman, when I was a little girl. But I felt the continuous pull and intense love that enfolded me, coming from their union. My mother told me later that my father was at first sad that I was not born a male child. But she also told me how pleased she was at how swiftly that disappointment vanished in his love for me, his child by her.

I sometimes thought that his games were too rough. But I quickly learned never to complain, because I wanted so much to see his smile, to hear his honest, deep laughter. The pony he gave me, on the day I reached my sixth spring, became the most cherished of my animals and playthings. She was a little beauty. Her coat was the color of a fawn and her mane was white. I named her "Gruel", because her colors were so like my daily porridge and milk. Within a year, with my father's careful training, I was able to ride as well as any warrior at Tintagel, though not as swiftly.

✿

To celebrate my seventh spring, my father called his vassal lords to Tintagel for a great feast. I was still the only child. I had already noticed how the ladies who became wives grew big with child, each year. But not my mother. Much later, I learned why. She did not want another child, and she had taken the rye cock's spur to abort each pregnancy.

I remember how proudly my father moved by my mother's side at my birthday feast. But she--usually so vivid and so direct--behaved rather shyly, even cautiously, when the visiting lords addressed her. I learned later that they were all powerful men, leaders and warriors. In court, some were more graceful and courteous than others. But they, like their ancestors and their descendants, were all ruthless plunderers, barely able to conceal their pleasure in quarreling, fighting, and the rape of lands, things, and women.

I sat in my small chair near my parents and watched the jugglers and the acrobats. I could not understand very much of the bard's songs, but on that night I experienced my first deep enchantment with melody, with music. The singer's harp spoke to me--to that little girl Morgain--in a voice I have never forgotten. I fell asleep in my chair and awakened only when Laba carried me up to bed and kissed me goodnight. Then I slept, ever so sweetly.

✿

In the summer of my seventh year, life at Tintagel began to change. My father was often away for weeks and would return exhausted, often with battle wounds. Our castle became a fortress. Every woman and child was kept busy with the needs of the men my father led in those sudden outbreaks of war. My task was to fold the clean cloths needed for bandages. I sat with the women in their great workroom.

Once, from my room high in the castle, I watched as a swarm of warriors in strange battle-dress was put to rout by my father and his men. The battle raged through the twilight into the night, until I heard my father shout, "Uther's worms! Now they crawl!"

And then I watched as our men, carrying torches, hacked at the fallen enemy wounded, to make sure that none were left alive to be healed and fed by the people of Tintagel.

✿

That night my father, bandaged and resting, exulted in the successful rout of the attackers. He seemed young and very handsome again: his slender face, the black and silver of his hair and beard, the brilliant blue eyes, and the thin, beaked nose over that gentle mouth--O dear father, how I loved you!

I had been put to bed but I couldn't sleep. I looked to see that Laba was asleep and then crept out of my bed to watch all that took place below, in the great hall. The victory supper was noisy with shouts and the sound of fists thumping on the oak table. My mother wore a gown of that rare blue of the sky at noon.

My father and mother drank many cups of mead, gazing into each other's eyes as they sipped. Then I saw him stagger up from his chair. My mother got up to take his arm, and he whispered close to her ear. When they moved to the stairs leading up to the sleeping rooms, I quietly went back to my room, next to theirs. I fell asleep with that pure, floating feeling that children know when their parents are happy and loving.

☼

But my father's victory did not put an end to the wars. I learned why, years later, from Merlin.

☼

Something troubles me, at this moment. It is about how I must tell my story. What was told to me? And what actually happened to me?

Our bards sing of times long past, the lines of their songs engraved in their memories by daily repetition. Their teachers, the old men and women who can no longer travel from village to village, correct every twist of memory. In this, my story, I must call on my own memory. But many things that affected my life were told to me, yet did not happen to me. My mother never talked to me about wars and the other affairs of men.

It was Merlin who later tried to help me understand how what happened outside my own experience nevertheless touched my life and, in some deep fashion, changed the axis of my growth. Despite all that happened between us, I am grateful to him for many things, especially during the years of our intimacy, so long ago.

And I am grateful to him for the teachings that armed me to become his antagonist. Hail, Merlin! Old friend, lover, magician, enemy. I know you sleep somewhere like an old bear, making yourself young again for the tasks you will face in the coming span of your years.

I shall speak only the truth, as I know it. As I scan the tapestry of memory, I can feel in myself the little girl, Morgain, and the young woman, Morgain--all those Morgains who continue to live inside my skin. It is sweet, but also bitter.

✿

To continue. For about a month there had been no alarms at Tintagel. The castle was really a fortress, with the ocean guarding the rear and great earthwork barriers in front.

My father spent those peaceful days with his lieutenants and soldiers to keep their spirits high and to sharpen their training in the skills of fighting on horse and on foot.

At that time the Romans, who had invaded and captured Britain some years before, had appointed Lord Uther as the Pendragon, the overlord of the Briton's landholder lords.

Uther Pendragon! How that name makes my guts quiver with hatred even now! Uther's chief lieutenant was a huge man, Lord Ulfius. Ulfius had been a friend to my father but had sworn fealty to Uther a year before.

Ulfius had visited with us many times. I remember how he would seat me on his huge, booted foot and rock me up and down as he made snorts and hoofbeat sounds, holding my hands in his huge, hard-skinned ones. I would laugh with delight until he would set me gently down, smiling into my eyes with the affection of a man who had no children he could call his own but who warmly wished for them.

And I also remember how Ulfius's boot made a delicious tickling and heat in the fork of my thighs as he lifted me and lowered me, again and again. It was the first time that I had felt something different from the wet, warm pleasure of pissing, in that private, miraculous part the Great Mother gives to all women.

I remember how, when Ulfius had left us to join Uther's court, I tried to give myself that pleasure with my hand. And I remember that it was not the same.

☼

Years later, I learned from Merlin that Ulfius had told Uther about my mother--that she was beyond all other women in grace and beauty, a woman who would burn the mind and guts of any man who looked at her. Uther Pendragon was a lecher. So Merlin, Uther, and Ulfius devised a scheme to enable Uther to see Ygraine with his own eyes.

Uther sent a messenger to Tintagel, offering a truce. My father was invited to attend a feast at Uther's Cadbury Castle to demonstrate his acceptance of the truce. I was too young to know anything of this at the time, of course. But I do remember how alone I felt, and the tears I tried to hide as I saw my mother and father ride away from Tintagel to Cadbury Castle.

✿

It was after my mother's passing that Lady Ceinwen told me of that fateful meeting. When Uther Pendragon greeted my parents he behaved with the grace befitting the meeting of two lords of high estate. To my father, Uther expressed his concern for the wounds he had suffered. With my mother Uther was courteous but distant.

At the feasting table Uther sat in the center, with my father at his right and my mother and Lady Ceinwen at his left. Ceinwen could see that, as my father grew more at ease with the good mead and food, Uther turned more frequently to address my mother, at first in the gracious manner of a considerate host, and then to speak softly and even whisper to her.

Ceinwen observed Ygraine's blush at one of Uther's whispered remarks. Ceinwen said she could see the glittering stare of a hunter stalking its prey as Uther whispered with his full, shiny lips into my mother's ear.

Later, after the bards had sung, Uther arose to end the night's revels. He again addressed my father respectfully and urged him to accept a place in the ranks of British lords sworn to govern and defend their lands under his, the Pendragon's command. My father was rather unsteady when he replied, but he made no oath of fealty. He thanked Uther for his courtesy, and my mother held him firmly by the arm as they walked out of the hall to their rooms.

Lady Ceinwen heard Ygraine tell my father how Uther had behaved--that Uther's truce was offered not only to seal a compact of fealty but also to bring her to Uther's bed. Ygraine told my father that Uther had urged her to come to his bedchamber after Gorlois had fallen asleep; how his words had become increasingly coarse as she disregarded his praise of her beauty and his desire to see her naked.

My father would have given his life to protect my mother. So it was with great difficulty that she persuaded him not to confront Uther immediately. Then she expressed her fear that neither she nor Gorlois were safe at Cadbury and urged him to leave Uther's castle before the coming dawn. Lady Ceinwen helped them, as cleverly as ever. By the break of day they were well on the road back to Tintagel.

I remember how my nurse squeezed my hand in her delight at seeing my father and mother at the head of the little procession returning to Tintagel. We were standing at the very top of the main tower. Laba lifted me up so that I could see better. I had become accustomed to my father's frequent absences. But this was the first time that both my parents had left me and I can feel even now that delicious quivering of my heart as their faces slowly and steadily grew larger in my vision.

I was hugged, fondled, and kissed. I noticed a difference in the smell of my mother's skin when she held me close after she dismounted in the courtyard. Her sweat was spicy and made my nose prickle. I told her this after her bath and she smiled and tweaked my nose.

✧

The next morning one of my father's spies arrived at the castle. I understood, from the manner with which my father listened to the lad and the urgency of his questions, that Tintagel was in danger again. My father called his lieutenants, the villagers were alerted by the drummers atop the tower, and by noon a heavily armed party left Tintagel under my father's command. The castle became a fortress once more.

Again, all the ladies of the castle were assembled in the great workroom. I sat close to my mother's chair folding the clean bandage cloths, while the other girls helped the women mix the healing salves and cook the soups and meats for the survivors when they returned from battle.

My mother was unusually quiet all that day. When our eyes met I could sense her approval; but I could not win the smile that usually came with her glance. So I knew that she was troubled and I tried to be very diligent in my task. I remember the flinty edge of Ygraine's voice when dear Ceinwen accidentally tipped and spilled a pitcher of the precious comfry potion--and Ceinwen's mute, downcast face as she listened to Ygraine's scalding words. We worked in whispers and silence for the rest of that day.

☼

At sundown (how I love that miraculous bridge between day and night!) we could see the blackening sky divided by thick threads of lightning. Gradually all the hissing, ripping, and rumbling of the storm grew louder, rushing from over the sea to drench the castle itself. We worked on in torchlight, and after supper Ygraine ordered the women to retire for the night. I kissed and hugged her very tightly before I went off to my room with Laba.

☼

I cannot remember ever being frightened of thunder and lightning, as so many women are. I remember being held in my father's arms at Tintagel as we looked out on those raging skies, how he exclaimed with delight at each snap and crash of lightning and thunder, and praised the torrents of rain and hail. Below us, the ocean smashed into the tall rocks and sent spumes high enough to make great white sheets of water. With my father I learned to delight in--to live in--every manifestation of earth and sky, water and fire. So after Laba had fallen asleep, I left my bed and went to the window slit to watch the wild storm.

The sea and land were visible only when the lightning blazed its ragged streaks from the sky to the earth and the ocean. I saw a ribbon of lightning strike an oak tree in the small grove at the edge of the village, and I saw the tree split and burst into flames and fall. The fire was quickly doused by the drowning rain.

The storm subsided suddenly. Now great, long grey ropes of cloud pulled away to uncover a full moon. The cold wind made my eyes tear, so I wrapped my sheepskin all about me from head to toe, and I sat watching the heaving, quicksilver ocean, wondering.

My wondering state was broken by an unlikely sound, the clopping of horses' hooves down below. I strained to look down from my window slit and saw three armored men on their horses.

I could not see their faces, only the tops of their helmets--but one of them carried a lance flying the blue and white of my father's pennant. I felt such delicious joy! My father was safe!

I dropped my sheepskin and quietly went to the door between my room and my parents', opening it just enough to peek through to see my father come home.

I had secretly observed my father and mother many times before, at first in awe of their strange sounds and their heaving bodies. But by now, a girl past her eighth birthday, I had learned that men and women coupled sometimes like the animals in our barns and fields, and sometimes face to face. We called it "enjoying" each other.

Now I waited to see my father safely home and going to bed with my mother. Silver shafts of moonlight, formed by the window slits, patterned their bed and the corners of the room. The air was gentle, fresh, and sweet after the storm.

My mother was still asleep when their door opened. The man wore my father's leather armor, but he seemed larger than my father. I felt a quick thrust of fear in my belly as I watched my mother stir, sensing another's presence. She whispered, "Gorlois?"

The man grunted, keeping his back turned to her as he shed his battle suit. Now I knew for certain that he was not my father, for the hair on his body glistened brown and auburn, not black. My body began to shake with cold, blind fear, and my throat became as dry as a bone.

When the man turned toward the bed my mother whispered, "Gorlois?" again.

Then I saw that the man carried leather thongs and a wide leather strap. His cok was large and stiff. He moved very swiftly to smother my mother's startled cry with both hands, pressing the leather strap over her mouth. She thrashed wildly, but he straddled her, locking her waist between his knees. I could not see her face, but I saw her hands clawing at his beard, and then I saw him tie first one and then her other wrist to the bed posts.

He slid back over her legs and slowly opened her gown. Then I heard his deep moan as he stared at her uncovered body. Her legs continued to thrash under him until he lifted them and forced his shoulders under her knees. After a moment, he thrust himself into her. I watched, terrified and blinded by the unbearable, hot fear in my belly as he began to rock himself in her, just a few times. Then I heard those deep, helpless moans that I have learned are the body's song that marks the absolute, inescapable climax of absolute, inescapable desire. He slowly collapsed on her body as her legs slid down from his wet, glistening shoulders. After what seemed only a few moments, she slowly raised her legs again and clasped them around his waist to pulse her body against his.

When her soft moans and rippling movements subsided he pulled himself heavily away to sit at the edge of the bed. He turned his head to allow his eyes to caress the curves and shadows of her quiet body. Then he went to the heap of his clothes. When he had dressed himself he returned to the bed and untied one of her wrists.

I heard him whisper, "I shall have you, Ygraine," and he walked out of the room.

I have never understood why I had stayed at the door, shivering, silently watching that secret, wild coupling.

My fear? Or my fascination? Why had I been unable to make even the slightest cry or whimper?

I ran back to the window slit in my room. One of the men below, staring at the quiet, heaving ocean, was standing so motionless that he seemed to be in a dream. His nose, forehead, cheeks, and chin seemed carved from a block of silver. Suddenly he turned to look up to the castle tower, the moonlight flashing for a moment in his eyes. Then he greeted the man who had just left my parents' bedchamber.

The third man laughed quietly as he looked up at my parents' window slit, and I recognized the face of Ulfius, our former friend, as he too greeted the man who had just enjoyed my mother. After a gruff exchange with our guards, Tintagel soldiers, the three men mounted their horses and rode away.

I went into my parents' bedchamber. My mother was sitting up in the bed, and she asked what I was doing awake in the middle of the night. I told her that I had been frightened and that I thought my father had come home. She motioned to me to come into her bed. She stroked my hair and told me not to worry because my father would return very soon. I wanted to, but I could not bring myself to ask about the man I had seen in her room. Again, I remember the spicy smell of her sweat, now mixed with Uther's, as I fell asleep close to her warm body.

☼

Two days later my father's body was carried into the great hall at Tintagel. His lieutenant, badly wounded himself, told us how my father had been trapped and killed in an ambush by Uther's men, who cut him down like a stag in the forest. The lieutenant, Sir Girald, wept as he told of my father's cold, savage bravery, alone in the surrounding circle of his slaughterers.

My mother's face was wet with tears as she tried to calm Girald's rush of bitter words. Then she rose to give orders to the servants, who carried my father on the pallet to the Druid's table under the sacred oak.

I was not allowed to come close to him until the late afternoon. He had been wrapped in a shroud that covered every part of his body except for a slit for his closed eyes, and another for his terribly slashed, folded hands. I was ill with grief, and Lady Ceinwen comforted me all that day with cold wet cloths while she murmured her sorrows with mine.

At twilight our Druid gave my mother a sprig of mistletoe to place in my father's wounded hands. He was tied into the slender, black boat. Then our Druid made the gestures of reassurance to the departing voyager, and we watched at the edge of the sea as the Druid pushed the boat away and the currents carried my father to the Otherworld.

The waters were dull and heaving slowly. Thin streaks of lightning began to chase each other under the heavy clouds, far offshore. Suddenly, their wild, blazing bolts split open the knowledge within me that I hated Uther, that I would kill him if I were brave and powerful. I hated him, and with their lightning my goddesses offered me the strength to wish him dead.

☼

Uther sent a delegation of courtiers to Tintagel to express his sorrow at the death of Gorlois and the proposal to share his life and fortunes with Ygraine, because of his love for her.

My mother received the delegation graciously and asked that she be allowed to consider Uther's offer. She promised to respond within seven days. Her marriage to Uther Pendragon took place at Uther's Cadbury Castle, about two months after my father's death.

I cannot explain the child Morgain's inner knowledge that my mother would accept Uther as husband. Yet I knew that she would, from the music of her voice when she told me of Uther's offer.

Now, as I speak from the woman Morgain, I can understand why she may have agreed to the marriage. Ygraine knew that Uther was a man--a warrior--so powerfully commanded by his lust and ambition that she would never be allowed peace if she rejected him. And Uther's lust had revived her own. I now know too well what that experience, what that wild enjoyment is, to be disdainful or contemptuous of it in any woman. And I do not think that Ygraine could have remained alone, at peace at Tintagel with the memories of Gorlois resounding in all its rooms and corridors.

✪

Cadbury Castle was a great structure, much larger than the castle at Tintagel, so our ladies and servants and a few of our warriors settled into it quite comfortably. Uther had issued precise instructions for my mother and her attendants to be accepted as equals in his own court. We were treated with grace, as members of Uther's family.

At first I was unhappy with the room given to me at the end of the hall of bedchambers, so far away from my mother's. Laba, my nurse, had some difficult times with me, but Lady Ceinwen was always sympathetic and soothing.

At that time Ceinwen was a young woman of about twenty-five years, very blonde and fair--skinned, with a gaunt, bony face and a delicious odor. Her mother was my father's sister. After her parents were killed in one of the vicious Pict raids on Meare, dear Ceinwen came to live here at Tintagel under my father's care.

Ceinwen is a weaver, and some of her tapestries were brought from Tintagel to decorate and warm my mother's rooms at Cadbury. Ceinwen would distract and entertain me with the stories she had woven into her tapestries, pointing to the people, the flowers, the trees, and the animals. I remember those stories well, and I have a few of those tapestries at Tintagel now--

"The Lady Imprisoned," "Fishermen at Meare," "The Boy and the Fox."

I learned to weave tapestries from Ceinwen. My mother had instructed her to teach me during our first winter at Cadbury. Ceinwen taught me with her patience, with her love for color and design, and her cleverness in making stories for the tapestries she wove. My own were quite small at first. Working with the colored threads, I too could make my own stories out of my dreams and wonderings. I love weaving above all the crafts I know.

Ceinwen and I carefully kept my first tapestry in a wooden chest during its progress, so that we could reveal it complete to my mother. When my mother saw it for the first time in the springtime of the following year her expression changed very suddenly from pleasure to barely concealed dismay.

The story I had woven was "A Battle at Tintagel." My father, carrying his blue and white pennant, leading his warriors and routing the enemy. The warriors all simple twig-figures around the castle at Tintagel, the high rocks and the sea below.

Uther, who was sitting with my mother when I brought the finished tapestry to her, glanced at it, and bent closer. Then he turned and for a moment stared at me with ice in his eyes. He burst into a roar of laughter, shouting "Good! Very good, little one!" and he arose from his chair and stamped out of the room. Ceinwen told me, years later, of the bitter scolding she received from my mother for having guided me in making such a story.

But I had already learned that Ceinwen was my friend and ally, and that she had found a simple, short thread to bridge the years between our birth days.

✡

Uther Pendragon was a huge man, dominating in all his parts. Even if he had not been a great leader and warrior, he would have commanded attention by his appetites for pleasure, conflict, and conquest. A few months before he wedded my mother his previous wife had been killed by a young horse that she had been training. Uther was not a man who could live without the enjoyment of women. Now he clearly adored my mother, both simply and as a mark of his prowess--as his captive.

In my new home with its large staff, appropriate for the household of the commander of all the Britons, I behaved timidly at first. Uther's immense, roaring speech frightened me. But some of the men, Uther's friends and advisers, did put me at ease when Uther was not present.

Lord Ulfius tried to win me to his affection again with stories of his old friendship with my mother and father. But I could not erase my memory of his smiling face in the moonlight at Tintagel, just a short time ago. So I was shy with him and did not allow him to play the old games with me.

The Druid who conducted the rites of marriage was the other man who had waited at the Tintagel gate, while Uther enjoyed my mother. I recognized him instantly. Again, seen closer, his face seemed molded of silver. I was presented to him on the morning of the wedding day. He looked down at me, isolating me from all the others around us, nodded his head, and said in his quiet, shining voice, "Welcome, Morgain. I shall be your friend. You shall call me Merlin."

The women of high place in Uther's court were of course the ladies in attendance to Uther's previous wives. They were at first distant but courteous to the women who came from Tintagel with us. But my mother quickly won their respect and obedience, loosening their stiffness by her gracious, unafraid affection. Ygraine was a leader among women, even to my little girl's eyes. She chided only for neglect or indifference, and she understood and permitted just the right range of gaiety or silliness.

☼

So the cloud over my spirit in those early days at Cadbury was slowly blown away. I began to enjoy each day. The mornings riding Gruel over the new inland country; the midday's work helping in the great kitchen; and the afternoons weaving in my room with dear Ceinwen.

Among the children at Cadbury was a little girl, just a few years older than I, whom I wanted to befriend. Her name was Morgause. She was one of Uther's children by his second wife. But I thought she was a fairy from one of Ceinwen's stories. She moved effortlessly, floating wherever she stepped. Her eyes were as green as young grass, and it seemed that her skin had been made from the tints of apples. Her long hair was so blonde that it was almost white. Even though her voice was oddly harsh, I thought her the most beautiful person I could ever imagine, and I waited each day with excitement at the prospect of her coming into the workroom.

At first Morgause and I were polite and cautious with each other. But we swiftly moved closer as we learned how many pleasures we shared, with only one exception. Morgause dreamed of becoming a great lady, wedded to a powerful lord and mothering many children. I could not imagine myself ever wishing for such things. But our other shared pleasures--riding, learning the ways of the kitchen, telling stories, and listening at night to the harps and songs of the bards--these carried us far beyond the different dreams of our future lives.

Morgause and I were fascinated by Merlin, by both his person and his free movement throughout the court and castle. We knew that he was Uther's Druid, of course. But Morgause and I spoke only to each other of his airy beauty. I remember some of the ways we tried to picture him in words:

"He is without thickness, only length and width, he came from a silver mother and a silver father, he can fly like a bird when he wishes, he knows everything that is known, he has never loved a woman, nor enjoyed one, his children are the trees, the grasses, flowers and stones, he can heal any wound and banish any stomach ache."

☼

On the sixth day of each week the children of the court assembled under the great Druid oak tree at the side of the castle. We sat in a half circle, our attention interrupted occasionally by burbles from the very young children. Merlin simply smiled at the noisemakers until they subsided into their own quiet, smiling attention.

Merlin told us the names and ways of trees, herbs, flowers, stones, and the small animals that he snared for these lessons. One day we moved to a barn where a cow had been striving for three days to drop its calf. After Merlin had explained what he was about to do, he reached, slowly and gently, into the cow's birth tube, pulling the calf's legs, timing his efforts with the cow's. We watched, absolutely silent, until the calf was thrust and then pulled into the air. We watched the cow nibble at the caul, and then we cried out with delight as the new brown and white calf raised and then dropped its pretty head. Merlin's gaze, as he watched the calf breathing its first air, was as gentle as when he looked at us.

☼

My mother was now big with her new baby. She moved more heavily and slowly, but she was very healthy and, indeed, happy. She would hold my hand on her belly to let me feel the curious, brief ripples inside. They alarmed me, at first. But very soon I found those signs of another, concealed life very exciting to touch and think about. I began to imagine a baby brother or sister, and Morgause and I would wonder about names, the size of its nose and ears, and the color of its hair and skin.

☼

One morning I awoke to my mother's loud cries. It had been a very warm summer, and the curtains over the window slits had been removed. My mother's cries seemed to echo inside and outside the castle, and while I dressed I thought everyone must know that the moment of my mother's birthing trials had come. Laba and I went out of our bedchamber into the corridor. We stood in the deep shadow, listening to my mother's cries coming from the opposite end of the corridor. Laba prevented me from moving with her strong hands clasping my shoulders.

Suddenly Merlin's door opened. As physician to the court, he had been awaiting the birthing of my mother's baby. Merlin rushed to my mother's room, came out and raced down the stairs into the great hall. Then I heard horse's hooves clopping impatiently.

I thought that Merlin had gone away, and I was frightened for my mother's safety. Her cries now came more often. There was one piercing scream, and then no more. My mother's bedchamber door opened, and I saw Muirinn, her midwife, come out of the room holding something in her arms. She walked to the stairs and down into the great hall.

Bewildered, I ran back to the window slit in my room. Below, I saw Merlin on his horse. Muirinn ran out and handed the little bundle up to him. He carefully placed it in a leather bag tied to his waist. He glanced up to the shaft of light from my mother's room, then goaded his horse and cantered out of sight.

Laba forcibly prevented me from going to my mother's room that night. Something very strange had happened. But Laba assured me again and again that I need not fear for my mother, that all was well. When I asked about the little bundle that Muirinn had carried out of my mother's bedchamber, Laba told me that there was nothing to be alarmed about and that this was not the time to disturb my mother. I went to my bed and wondered while tears wet my face. I understood nothing of what I had seen and heard.

I was allowed to visit my mother in the morning. There was no baby with her. She greeted me and told me that the child was still-born. She wept, and her sorrow made me weep with her. I tried to comfort her. I was so very sad because I would not have the brother or sister I had been waiting for. Then my mother, in her sweet kindness, said that I would remain her dearest and only child. Our cheeks pressed together, her tears mingling with mine.

☼

My mother recovered from the birthing within a few weeks. She spoke to me of learning the skills expected of a noblewoman, and told me that Merlin was to be one of my teachers. I could barely conceal my delight. My mother smiled, knowing how much I liked to be with the children when Merlin was teaching. Even at that age I knew Merlin had great knowledge and skill in many things, and I had seen how respectfully he was treated by my mother and by Uther himself.

My mother told me that I was to spend each morning with Merlin until the bell was sounded for the midday meal. I glowed in a place within myself, in anticipation. Lady Ceinwen was to continue teaching me the crafts, and in the late afternoons my training in horsemanship was to be under the guidance of Erec, the stable boy who cared for my pony, Gruel.

☼

Merlin's teaching began with a long walk outside the castle grounds. I remember that first morning so clearly!

As we walked he asked me what I liked most of all to do.

I replied, "Everything," and his quiet face was transformed by a smile.

Then he talked about meadow grasses and flowers, and very seriously about trees. He talked of trees as if they were the most wonderful signs of the presence of our gods, because of the way trees grew, reaching higher each year up to the sky. I learned their names, each so lovely to say and hear: the oak, the alder, the beech, the chestnut, the ash, the willow, the yew, the apple and the pear, and others. One of the most beautiful things I learned that first day was to watch the branches of trees as they were moved by the wind. The heavy rise and fall of oak limbs, the soft grace of the willow. We collected leaves from each tree for me to take to my room, so that I would be able to study and name them quickly.

I learned the names of the fruits and the berries, and when they were ripe for eating. I learned how to treat the mistletoe and its berries and how to use them as remedies for wounds and mild illnesses.

Sometimes my morning lessons were interrupted when Merlin was called to meet with Uther. I spent those mornings alone in my room, studying the things we had collected--stones, leaves, small dead animals, feathers, the pulps and seeds of fruits, and herbs. Do you remember how

I would roll their beautiful names in my mouth,
dear Ceinwen?

☼

I must interrupt myself here. Ceinwen, do
you think I should tell all the things Merlin taught
me?

You nod your head and smile.

Do you think women, and even men, can
learn those things from me?

Again you nod your head.

Well then, as you know, I believe that I
remember everything. There are some things I
shall want to take with me to the Otherworld
when I am ready for that voyage. I shall not tell
those things. But there are so many things that
you can tell me, dear Ceinwen! How I wish you
would break your vow, for just one day?

Now you shake your head, with that same
sad smile. Ceinwen!

☼

I was Merlin's morning pupil from the
spring of my eighth year until I entered my sixteenth. Even then, as now, I knew that his teachings could have continued for years to come. He
was, he is, eternally wise. I think he holds all the
wisdom of the world in his brain and heart.

These are some of the important things I
learned from dear Merlin. To breathe deeply,

always keeping one corner of my attention on my breathing. To love, truly love, all living things, because I, too, am in the great wheel of life, death, rebirth. That only the forms change, and what fills the forms remains the same, always the pull and thrust of male and female. That the nipples on a man's and a woman's chest are the oldest signs of our beginnings. Look at the warrior's shield, his protector, round as a breast with its thrusting nipple!

I learned to study all animals closely because they show us how men, women, and children move, behave, and think. I learned to recognize the inward qualities of men and women and children, by allowing them to sound within myself, with my own appetites, my dislikes, my own needs, and my ambitions.

To recognize the greatness that may reside under ragged clothing, and the meanness under the gold and purple. I learned that those who live between those two extremes are easy to control, because they are so often flabby, without form, and can be enticed to move in whatever direction I may will.

I learned the importance of the four winds. At night, under the sky, I learned from Merlin how to look at the great wheel of stars that turn around the axle of Polaris. He taught me the wonderful meanings of the signs of the zodiac.

He taught me to honor all my teachers for their knowledge. He taught me to be patient with children, because each one comes into the world from another, previous pair of lives that is different from any child's.

I learned that all speech has melody, and that while listening to others' conversations I might hear their pleasure in each other's company, or the despair that can be dispelled or reinforced, or the boredom and fatigue that arises from the unchanging sameness of their lives. And I have known the deep pleasure that comes with overhearing the melodies of mutual affection.

Merlin would entertain me by mimicking the cries of birds and bulls and cows, giving them the melodies of pleasure and boredom, fatigue and affection. He enjoyed provoking me to giggle, and I loved him for that.

I also learned how to throw a knife with precision, by practicing with stones at an apple and then with a pointed stick. I learned how to bandage an animal's wounded limb, so that I could bandage a person's limb more sensibly.

I learned how to squat and hunker, and never to allow waste to clog my bowels, to go to shit when my belly signaled me.

With Merlin I learned the making of perfumes, the scents that distinguish women from each other. And he taught me the exquisite pleasure of the laying on of hands.

That happened in the last winter of my lessons with him, in his room. It was in the winter of my sixteenth year, on a terribly cold day. He had warmed the room with a clean fire of logs that gave off a spicy fragrance.

Merlin fastened the bar locking his door. He had never done that before. He asked me to sit facing him on the sheepskin that lay in front of the fireplace.

His light blue eyes were unusually intense as he talked of the healing power of hands. He asked me to place my palms on his. I was startled by the sudden rush of heat coming up from his into my own. Then he asked me to try to do the same, placing his palms on top of mine. His palms were now cold, but I could not do what he asked.

He took my wrists in his hands and brought my palms slowly closer to the hot ashes at the front of the fire, then gradually away. He firmly insisted that I could make such a change by imagining and willing it.

Then he laid back on the sheepskin and asked me to sit astride his belly, straddling him, while he opened his shirt to reveal his chest. He reminded me that I already knew how sensitive the nipples are in men and women, and that I should try to pass the heat from my palms to his nipples.

I was very excited, and also bewildered by this new, intimate contact with him. I could feel a great heat flowing out of the fork of my thighs. I placed my palms on his nipples. Our gazes locked, and then Merlin moaned and asked me to close my eyes. He whispered that I was wonderful while he reached behind me to fumble with his smallclothes.

I felt his long, stiff cok slide easily into my cunnus. I remember my eyes opening in surprise to stare at him. Then he moved slowly and wordlessly within me to ascend to his and my ecstasy.

Dear Ceinwen, I see your cheeks flush as I tell you all this. But you couldn't have known everything. And what of your own life, what of your own enjoyment when you were young? You must know that I have always loved Merlin, that I will forever keep him in the secret place all women know.

But I must go on. Ceinwen, write!
You nod, "Yes," at last.

☼

Several times before that first enjoyment--that first enchantment--with Merlin, I had secretly enjoyed Erec, the groom. Merlin, with his miraculous sight, could have known that. You would not have known that. But you will understand.

At Cadbury Castle I had attended wedding ceremonies for the young daughters and sons of noblemen and ladies-in-waiting of the court. They were usually about my age, and I knew they would very soon discover the pleasure of enjoying each other. Alone in my bed on those nights I would feel the swelling pleasure in the fork of my thighs. Then I would burn with the need to know what enjoyment with a man could reveal to me.

Erec was--is!--about seven years older than I am. Each time we enjoyed each other he was full of terror at the possibility of being discovered as the debaucher of a young noblewoman. It was of course dangerous for him. But each time his terror quickly dissolved in the heat of his desire and my own intense curiosity.

The first time I enjoyed Erec was on a summer day after a wedding ceremony at the castle. We had gone for our daily ride into the forest near Cadbury and had entered a narrow, sunlit clearing. I suddenly halted, dismounted, and turned to smile at Erec. I took deep breaths of the air, it was so fragrant with the freshness of green leaves and mint, while Erec remained astride, looking down at me. He had always been shy and cautious as he helped me to mount my horse; his replies to my questions always came in short gasps; and I often saw him gazing at me with such anguished longing. I was sure that he knew that I wished to enjoy him.

In the dappled clearing I smiled at him while I undressed myself to nakedness. He closed his eyes for a long moment before he dismounted. Then, standing next to his lovely mare, he too shed his clothes. It was the first time that I had seen a naked man since that terrible night at Tintagel. Erec was beautiful then, so long ago!

I raised my arms to welcome him and he walked slowly to embrace me. I heard him groan and sob as we lay down in the warm grasses and leaves. When I asked about the tears that had come to his eyes, he shook his head and did not reply.

I felt his cok enter me. There was the sudden pain that my mother had told me I must expect, and then it disappeared as he began the slow, wonderful caresses inside my cunnus. He spent himself quickly in a throbbing shudder. Then he lay quiet on and inside my body. I remember how both strange and delicious it was to feel my sweat mingling with his, that first time.

I held him close while he kissed my throat and chin again and again. He whispered that he had loved me from the time he first saw me, when I was a little girl, and that he had dreamed over and over again of just such a moment. He did not ask if I loved him. He would have known that I didn't, and that I would not.

As we lay there I felt his cok stiffen in me again. He grasped my buttocks and made me move tightly against him until I heard myself whimpering and felt my inward, blinding pleasure rise and explode into a vision of spinning stars in a dark blue night sky. Now I knew.

We unlocked ourselves and I asked him to tell me what he saw. Before he could answer I turned my back to him. He paused before saying anything. But I felt his rough hand course slowly down from my shoulder to my arm, then reach for my hidden breast, then down the side of my waist and hip, and finally stop to press his hand in the cleft of my buttocks. At last he spoke. He said that he would always wish to see me with his eyes and his hands.

I turned to lie again on my back and folded my hands under my head. The back of my neck was wet with my sweat. I had never before known such sweet, deep peace in my body. But my mind raced on in curious whirls. I asked him, "And now?"

I watched his brilliant, ice-blue eyes while he studied, indeed touching every part of me with his gaze. He whispered again that I was the most beautiful woman he had ever seen, that I was far more wonderful than I was in his dreamings, and that he wished to kiss and taste every part of my body. I moved to suggest that I would like that.

With his lips and tongue he caressed my shoulders, my breasts, my belly, the fronds of hair at my fork, then along my thighs to my toes, and back up again. I smiled and asked if he liked me.

He raised his head to stare at me and said that he would die for me.

Although I have never said this to him, I have always been grateful to him. Erec was the first to show me my own body.

☼

But those few enjoyments with Erec had not prepared me for what happened that winter morning with Merlin. I had loved Merlin from the first times we went walking together when I was a child. He may have been secretly preparing me to become a Druid priestess. But I shall never know that for certain, nor did I wish for such a life.

☼

Uther Pendragon! Uther, leader of all the lords of my beautiful land. How he, even his name, frightened me when I was a child! Uther was a giant, larger than any of the warriors and lords of his court. His voice was huge, and he would enlarge it in his fits of rage. He paid the least possible attention to the children of the court. We scurried like mice to avoid his heavy, huge strides through the castle.

His burden, like his body, was huge. The Romans had selected him as the successor to Ambrosius, to be the Pendragon, the title he fought so hard to justify. The Roman army commanders were greatly impressed by Uther's ferocious strategies against the Picts, the Irish, and the Saxon invaders. In exchange for shipments of our grains, the Romans supplied Uther with metals to be fashioned according to their methods, into weapons, plows, and other tools.

It was told that Uther was ferocious in battle, and that disputes with his liege lords were most often settled by his boiling anger and roaring. We women were never permitted to appear in the chambers of the councils of lords, but Uther's bellowing was often heard throughout the castle before the councils had ended.

✿

Ygraine was the only person that Uther treated with gentle, adoring courtesy. I learned early to avoid him, and always to seem modest and shy when he addressed me directly. He frightened me and I hated him. But I was also secretly grateful for his absolute, unswerving love and respect for my mother.

During my twentieth year Uther's shaky reign began to unravel. He prodded the liege lords to muster larger numbers of young men into the army he was building. But the lords stubbornly resisted. They knew very well that converting strong, young farmers into warriors simply wasted their lands and crops. So the lords offered the least possible number of farmers' sons to serve in Uther's army.

The Picts' spies reported the squabbles among the British lords, and their raids grew more and more daring, and more often successful. After repelling one such raid Uther called a meeting of the lords at Cadbury Castle.

Such meetings were always preceded by a great feast, attended by the lords, their ladies and ladies-in-waiting, Uther's councilors and warrior lieutenants, and all their children. I sat near the head of the table next to Lady Ceinwen, who was always quietly at my mother's side.

I had observed the changes in my mother during these years. Her face was now lined with faint creases, and she moved more slowly. Her burdens had increased with Uther's desperate obsessions. Now, seated next to him, she placed her hand over his bandaged hand, wounded in the battle two days before, to calm him.

While Uther chewed at the roasted meats I saw his face grow redder, and the scars of old wounds on his forehead and cheeks become whiter. When he finished eating he arose, wiping his hands and mouth with his napkin. Then, standing fully erect at his great height, he bellowed for the attention of his guests.

I remember his words, for he had never spoken in that fashion before. He said that he was sick to the gills and tired in his skull, tired of the bickering that kept his forces barely adequate to defend Britain against the vulture Pict and Saxon raiders. Merlin and the bishop--Uther had recently submitted to the Roman pope's command that he adopt the Christian faith--looked up to stare at Uther. They, too, must have felt the tremors of his rumbling rage. I heard a curious noise in his breathing while the guests' chatter subsided into silence.

Uther's mouth opened to make words again, but only a strange, gargling sound issued from his lips. Suddenly, as if he had been struck a heavy blow across his back, he bent at the waist and crashed face forward on the table. Merlin stood quickly, moved to Uther and touched the side of his neck. Then he turned to us to say that Uther had passed on to the Otherworld.

My mother arose from her seat and placed her hand, briefly, on Uther's lifeless cheek. The bishop moved to Uther, made the sign of the cross and began to pray. An uproar of noisy words followed us as my mother, Lady Ceinwen, and I walked out of the great hall.

☼

Despite my mother's urging I had refused to accept the new Christian faith. With several other children of the court I had chosen to remain under the guidance of Merlin's Druid teachings. So Merlin and I stood together with those daughters and sons to watch the bishop administer the Christian rite of burial.

My mother remained in her room during the following week. Lady Ceinwen assured me each day that my mother was well but very tired. At the end of that week Lady Ceinwen came to tell me that my mother was sick and wished to see me.

I ran to her room and entered softly. Merlin was at her bedside and looked up at me.

Ygraine's eyes were closed when I whispered my greeting. Her mouth was slack and drooling. Merlin wiped her lips with a cloth and then Ygraine spoke my name and said that she was happy that I had come to her. I looked my question to Merlin, who slowly shook his head in reply.

I realized that my mother was dying. Lady Ceinwen, sitting at the far wall of the bedchamber, wept silently. Merlin asked me to excuse him from the room for a short time and I did so.

As soon as Merlin left the room my mother opened her eyes to look at me. She studied my face for a moment and then gestured with her fingers to come closer. In a whisper she said that I had a brother, that he was to become the new Pendragon, and then, "Merlin knows it all." Then she turned her tired face away and closed her eyes. Merlin reentered the room, and I told him that I thought my mother had passed over. He went to her and touched the side of her neck for a few moments. He turned to me and nodded slowly.

☆

At my mother's grave, just before she was lowered into it, I heard the bishop intone the words "dust unto dust, and ashes to ashes." I felt myself suddenly fill with anger at such solemnly spoken, utterly empty words. I knew that my mother would now embark on her journey into the Otherworld and that she would be filled with light. But I thanked the bishop for his kindness and swiftly turned away to walk alone in the meadow near the cemetery.

As I walked slowly among the lovely grasses I watched the way my steps pressed them flat to the earth. All those remembered experiences--the gift of my pony Gruel, my father's gentleness and intelligence, his terrible death, Uther's rape of my mother, their marriage, the teachings of Merlin and Ceinwen, the sudden passings of Uther and my mother--all began to weave a new tapestry in my mind's mirror.

I was now free for the first time in my life, free of the controls I had accepted with respect for my elders and teachers.

I had been offered the hands of several young men, sons of lords, in marriage. But I knew that their fathers were eager to become kin to the Pendragon and our ruling family. None of those callow, bashful youths could possibly have pleased me. So I had courteously expressed my reluctance to marry.

Now, although I was to remain at court, I resolved never to become a man's chattel, nor to submit to the disciplines and constraints imposed upon the other ladies of the court. I would respect, but not always obey, the new Pendragon, whoever that might be.

I continued my walk into the twilight. From just beyond the rise ahead of me I heard a raven's call, "Taw! Caw! Caw!"

In the hollow beyond the hillock a large raven was trying to lift itself into flight as it scuttled around in a tight circle. It beat the air with its right wing, and I saw that its left wing had been injured at the shoulder and was hanging uselessly. The skin and feathers were streaked with blood, and I saw the open wound as the bird continued its helpless flailing. The raven persisted in its circling motion, crying its "Caw!" again and again.

I hunkered down close to the bird. It looked at me fearfully, but it did not move away. I responded, echoing the raven's call quietly. I saw the glint of green feathers underneath its dense black coat. Suddenly the wounded bird glowed with beauty. As I continued to echo its "caws" I felt myself transformed. In those strange moments I had become a raven.

I gathered the bird into my arms. It pecked at my chest, but gently and tentatively. I carried it back to my workroom and washed the torn flesh at its shoulder. After I bandaged the wound I made a simple enclosure for it in one corner of the room. I set out a dish of water and another dish with small pieces of meat. It ate hungrily. I watched as it blinked and closed its eyes, wobbled slightly, and fell asleep. Then I called on my goddess to heal the raven's wing, as Merlin had taught me. I named the raven "Taw."

☼

What did Merlin know about a brother-- mine!--who would become the next Pendragon? My mother must have held many secrets, but this one was important to me and should have been revealed to me before she passed out of this life. I knew now that I must learn that secret from Merlin. I would tell him that I wished to enjoy him again.

I believe that I was the only woman in the court that Merlin enjoyed. I knew that Merlin practiced very intensely to control his lust. But we had not enjoyed each other for quite a number of months past, and now, in midsummer, I was becoming increasingly aware of the stirrings in my own body. They seemed somehow connected with my wish to overcome my sadness at my mother's passing. Merlin agreed to meet me again in the oak forest, in our trysting place.

I was the first to arrive at the forest grove. I had brought a basket of fruits and a jug of mead, which Merlin truly loved. The air was wonderfully hot and still. A lark sang and was answered by the twitterings of his audience of birds. Merlin silently helped me pull my dress over my head to uncover my nakedness. Then, while he slowly caressed every part of my body with his eyes, he undressed himself. We embraced, still silently, and began the miraculous play of enjoying each other.

Descending from our ecstasy, we fell into deep sleep in each other's arms, it seemed for just an instant, or an age. I was awakened by Merlin's voice close to my ear, and I heard him ask me to trace with my eyes the threads of mistletoe winding through the great oak's branches overhead. He bit into one of the ripe pears I had brought to the grove.

In the stillness, I moved my gaze along one thin vine. I felt Merlin's finger begin the delicious, slow traverse over my belly, knowing how the tingle would spiral toward my navel. I felt the quiver of almost unbearable pleasure, and I heard my inner voice tell me that the pleasure was so unspeakably delicious because it was Merlin who caused it, Merlin who loved me so completely and unquestioningly.

My inner voice rose to my throat with a moan, and then out of my lips, asking what my

life might have been if my father had been victorious over Uther, whether we would be lying together in this place now. I felt the sudden lift of
Merlin's finger away from my belly, and then he
poked it directly into my navel.

He moved his hand to my cheek to turn
my face toward his. With our noses almost
touching, his eyes smiled into mine. He said that
I should not play the what-if game, that it leads
nowhere because what has already happened
cannot be changed. He said that the memory of
the past is useful only to uncover the threads of
one's fate, and that we are given memory so that,
in the present, we may be able to shape the
future.

Unknowingly, Merlin had alerted me to
my own, secret purpose. I asked him what might
happen now that Uther had passed over, who
could become the new Pendragon?

Merlin did not answer. He sipped several
times from the jug of mead. Then he said that he
knew what Ygraine had wanted to tell me when
he had left her bedchamber on the night of her
passing, and that she did not wish me to be
ignorant of that knowledge. He was silent again
for a long time. I did not press him. There was
a half-smile on his face as he continued to think.
I closed my eyes and watched the hot pink glow of

sunlight coming through my eyelids, waiting, for I knew now that Merlin would tell me what he thought I should know.

He spoke of how he had cherished me as I grew from maiden to woman. That he had always known deep in his being that if he were ever to love a woman completely, he would have to be willing to use the dark magic to help his beloved move to the highest light. The possibility of such surrender had alarmed him deeply. But his passion for learning and his devotion to our Druid beliefs had helped him to resist the loss of self that he believed was necessary to love a woman completely.

Now I understood the shell, the armor he had made for himself. And now I understood that I could pierce that armor by using my body.

I had been lying on my back, still naked, with my hands clasped under my head as I listened to him. I said nothing. I slowly turned away to lie on my side, so that he had to speak to my naked back. I had already experienced his heightened lust whenever he gazed at my buttocks and entered me as a bull would a cow.

He continued to speak. He told me how he had helped Uther to plan the enjoyment of my mother. I felt a silent, furious scream rush through me. Now I knew! But I did not move, speak, and I kept my back to him while he went on to tell how he had exacted a vow from Uther that the child of that coupling would be given to him, Merlin, to be reared in secret. Then he told me that the high council of Druids had charged him with the task of maintaining the Druid influence over the Roman Pendragons.

He told of his deep pain whenever he remembered Ygraine's sorrow at the loss of that child, and of his helplessness in the face of his obligation to the council of Druids. Now, he said, the child, a truly magical boy, had reached young manhood. He was now seventeen years old, and was named Arthur.

Arthur would soon perform a remarkable deed that Merlin had devised. The boy would recover, extract, a superb sword from a block of stone. Merlin had named the sword "Excalibur," and he had fashioned a device in a block of stone that would enable Arthur alone to accomplish that feat. Merlin explained that the name of the sword, in Latin, meant "out of the stone."

"How soon?"

"Within a month," Merlin replied.

The sun was directly overhead now, and I was wet with salty sweat. I heard Merlin whisper to me that I be his cow. I brought myself to my hands and knees, then turned my head to smile at him as he prepared to enter me.

In that enjoyment, I had achieved my first victory over Merlin.

✿

I had learned that the best time for riding was in the early morning, shortly after sunrise when the air was fragrant with the dew and my horse was fresh and eager. A few days after my tryst with Merlin I rode to the pond in the stone quarry to bathe and swim in the crystal waters. While I dried myself I could hear the chinking sound of a chisel on stone coming from an open shaft in the quarry.

I was puzzled. I saw no horse tethered nearby, nor any sign of another person, no clothes at the edge of the pond, nothing. The chinking of the chisel continued. I became anxious for my own safety so I did not go to the open shaft to learn more. I mounted my horse--dear Ceinwen, do you remember her, Mabon, what a splendid animal!--and rode back to the castle.

Early the next morning, in the grey light before sunrise I went on foot to the quarry. A soft mist covered the meadow and the path. I thanked my goddesses for guarding my walk to uncover the secret in the quarry.

Again, there was no sign of the presence of another person. No sound came from the shaft. I had brought a torch with me and lit it from a flame of twigs I kindled with my flint and stone. Then I entered the shaft.

Instead of the tunnel I expected to see, the shaft led almost directly into a large cave. I immediately knew that this place was one of Merlin's secret workrooms. There were some picks, chisels, and two mauls; near one wall there were some open jars.

A white stone block sat majestically in the center of the floor. It had been carved to look like a natural boulder, narrow at its top, and reaching to the height of my knees. A thin, deep slit had been chiseled in the top surface, and three very narrow, deep holes had been cut into the sides.

I looked at the stone for some time and then the flash of understanding came to me. This was the stone from which Arthur--and only Arthur, my brother--would extract the great sword Excalibur, "out of the stone." The deep, narrow holes in the sides of the stone held the locking device. And Arthur would be instructed by Merlin to grasp the hilt of the sword in such a way as to unlock it from the stone. Excalibur, the sword itself, was the key to the lock.

As I walked around the stone, marveling at Merlin's craft, I saw a reflection of my torch light on the surface of something in one of the bowls. I went to it and saw my face and the torch mirrored on the substance in the bowl.

Merlin had told me about quicksilver and warned me that it was dangerous, poisonous.

I was very excited. I took a small, empty bowl from the stack against the wall, poured some of the quicksilver into it and went out of the cave. I carefully carried the bowl back to the castle, unseen by anyone. I set the bowl on my work table. I remember how the rising sun sent its golden rays through the window slits while I prepared to study the quicksilver.

Taw, my raven, was waiting for me. His wound had healed, but the wing remained useless and dragged on the floor as he approached me. I told him to come closer and stay by my side.

☼

Ladies of the court received bronze mirrors as giftes from their husbands. The mirrors came to us among the supplies sent from Rome. But the reflections they gave back to us were dull and without color. In the quicksilver mirror I was able to study my hazel eyes, the thin nose so like my father's, and the tight curls in my auburn hair.

I stared at myself for a long time, then fell asleep in my chair. I had never done that before. In my dream I saw myself looking into the quicksilver, watching people, my horse, my raven, and trees, especially willows, and how their branches shifted their shapes so smoothly in the wind. I saw my will--my willows!--changing the behavior of the people and animals that I summoned to the mirror.

I awakened to the sound of the castle bell that called us to midday dinner, but my dream remained almost fearfully clear. Taw had remained standing close to my chair while I dreamed. I stroked the back of his head while I thought about my dream.

Awake, I would try to use the mirror, as I had dreamed, by calling to the mirror those I wished to see. Then, if I could press my will into them, I might make them do whatever I might wish.

Later that day I was almost feverish with my impatience to learn how to use the quicksilver mirror. I dropped stones and flower petals and twigs on the shining surface. But all I could see was my own face. Then I thought of leaves, and how they change as they grow older, from green to golds and reds and browns.

When I dropped a fresh green leaf of mistletoe on the quicksilver the image of my face disappeared, and I could see whatever was happening at that very moment anywhere in the castle. I saw the cooks sweating in the castle kitchen, and Gwynn nursing her three-day-old daughter, and you, dear Ceinwen, at work on your tapestry frame. Wherever my mind turned, I could observe the scene in my mirror.

Then I wondered if I could see what might happen at some future time. Nothing, no object, no feather, nor gemstone, no eggshell, nothing shifted the image forward from the present to a future time.

Then I thought of trying an old, brown, dry mistletoe berry. The berry dissolved and made a fine dust on the surface. Now I saw shifting figures and scenes, but they were not in the future. I singled my attention to one scene. Merlin and Uther sat facing each other, in conversation. I saw their lips and jaws moving, but I heard nothing.

I knew now that the dry, brown mistletoe berry was the key to unlocking visions in the bowl of quicksilver. In that month I spent every evening at the mirror to master its gifts.

☼

You, Ceinwen, were the first that I called to my mirror. Did you know that? So many years ago! Do you remember that summer, after my mother's passing, how you sat at your loom, and how you arose to stare out of the window slit because you were certain that you heard the children playing in the courtyard near the stables, a place forbidden to them?

It was I and my mirror that made you do that. You were the first, and I chose you because you were, you are, the dearest of all to me. I did not trouble you after the second time, when you told me that you had experienced a strange force that made you interrupt what you were doing and move to something else, and that you wondered if you were becoming sick in your mind.

Dear Ceinwen! You look at me with so sweet a smile, even after I have told you all this. I love you. You are my other mother. But we must continue, and you must write everything I have just said about you, too.

☼

With the passing of Uther and my mother I had become the lady who was expected to manage the household affairs of the castle.

Many of the liege lords had come there to settle the naming of Uther's successor. Their noisy, snarling squabbles increased my contempt for the ways used by men to settle affairs of power. I decided that I did not care to be their housekeeper, despite my elevated status.

I was never at ease in housekeeping tasks and rarely able to give them my full attention. My mother's ladies-in-waiting had become mine, and I had instructed them to obey Lady Ceinwen in all such matters. As usual, Ceinwen behaved with utmost grace and swiftly won their obedience and trust.

✧

Lord Ulfius, once my father's and then Uther's chief counselor, was now an old man, the senior of the liege lords. He tried to subdue their vicious arguments, urging them to wait for decisions from Rome regarding the choice of the new Pendragon. They treated him with barely concealed indifference. But they hid their anger when the Bishop and Merlin were present. I had observed often enough that the lords were respectful only to those who represented superior political or spiritual power.

I had begun to think that I should, indeed that I deserved to, share in the power of the next ruler of the Britains. As Ygraine's daughter and the stepdaughter of Uther, the Pendragon, how could I be satisfied with the status of housekeeper?

Erec, who continued to care for my horse, had been chosen by Lord Ulfius to be one of his squires. I remained fond of him, although I no longer wanted him for enjoyment. But I encouraged his devotion by asking him to serve as my spy, to report to me the discussions that took place in the councils.

During their council meetings Erec would sit quietly with the other squires close to the chamber wall, all ready to serve the lords' needs instantly. Each morning, while he readied my horse, he reported to me what the lords had discussed and argued about.

Erec loved me, I knew that.

☼

A fortnight after I discovered the white stone in the secret quarry cave, Merlin addressed an angry gathering of the liege lords. He said that he knew his words might disturb some of them, but he wished to be heard without interruption. He asked Lord Ulfius and the bishop to share the duty of maintaining order.

Merlin's somber manner impressed the lords, and they agreed to remain quiet while he spoke.

Calmly, Merlin told them that a strange event had taken place. Behind the new church in the village of Pilsdon, less than an hour's ride to the east, a white stone had appeared, jutting out of the earth. He said that the stone was pierced by a sword of great quality and beauty, and that its hilt was engraved in Latin with the words: "He who shall extract this sword from this stone is the rightful king of Britain."

The lords exploded with shouts of disbelief, wonder, and frustration. The bishop held up his hand to stop their noise. Merlin, again calmly, explained his plan. Each lord must try to extract the sword from the stone. The lord who succeeded in this trial would become king. The bishop arose to ask the lords to engage in this effort with reverence, because this trial must have been ordained by God, who had placed the sword and stone on church ground. The assembly was stunned.

A brief silence was broken by Lord Ulfius, who asked how soon the trial could begin. Merlin looked to the bishop, who replied that it should begin that very day. The lords immediately ordered their squires to make ready for the journey to Pilsdon.

The entire company departed from Cadbury Castle by midmorning. I watched the solemn procession from my window slit. I had always enjoyed the manner of men riding, and these men were the finest on horse in all of Britain. Their squires held their lords' colored pennants high on that brilliant, sunlit day, and I saw another tapestry design take form in my mind's mirror.

In my room at the castle I sat at my quicksilver mirror, observing Merlin's trial in the Pilsdon churchyard. Of course none of the lords would be able to pull Excalibur out of the stone. I watched all of them make their furious, vain attempts. It was amusing to see such heroic, abysmal frustration.

Lord Cai was one of the younger lords who had come to the castle for the test. He represented his father, Lord Auctor, who owned great tracts of land and forest that he managed with great care. Cai was another brute of a man, but with a fine humor about his own bumbling, bearishness in the skills of horsemanship and armed combat.

☼

I did not know at the time that Cai's young squire was my brother, Arthur. Merlin told me later how he had taken the infant child of my mother and Uther to Lord Auctor's household, to be reared to become the king of all the Britons.

At first, Lord Auctor had resisted accepting so great a responsibility. But Merlin respected Auctor for his great skills as a farmer, a husband, and father, and was able to enlist him in carrying out his plan. He told Lord Auctor that the plan to prepare the boy Arthur to become the future king had been devised by the high council of Druids. The Druids were now determined to stand against Rome's feeble government of Britain, and especially against the growing power of the Roman Christian church officers.

So Lord Auctor, because he held strongly to the Druid faith, agreed to raise the boy in his household. Merlin told me that his choice of Lord Auctor was one of the best deeds in his life as a Druid.

Later, Merlin was able to persuade the bishop to accept the knowledge that a future king was being nurtured in secret, here in Britain. The bishop may have agreed to trust Merlin because of his own chafing impatience with the church councils far away in Rome. So he too became Merlin's ally in the scheme.

☼

Erec told me how Lord Cai, to prepare for his trial with the sword in the stone, had removed his belt and sword and his outer clothing. He tried mightily to pull Excalibur free of the stone, grunting and bellowing and swearing in his frustration. After his third try, drenched in sweat, he turned away, dressed and went off to drink mead with the other lords.

The lords' return from Pilsdon was joyless and leaden. The choice of a successor to Uther had not been resolved, and they were sullen and irritable at having being drawn into such a strange test. The company was at the midpoint of the journey back to Cadbury Castle when Lord Cai furiously exclaimed that he had forgotten to buckle on his sword belt before leaving Pilsdon. The lords jeered at him while Cai shouted at his squire, Arthur, to go back to Pilsdon and fetch his sword. When the company arrived at Cadbury they set to drinking and carousing and ribaldry with their wives and other women of the court.

Erec excitedly told how Arthur had returned from Pilsdon with Excalibur and immediately gave it to Lord Cai. Arthur said that he had searched the grounds of the Pilsdon church but found no trace of Lord Cai's sword or scabbard. He was drawn to the sword in the stone, he said. Because he was alone, he grasped its hilt and was astonished at the ease with which he drew Excalibur out of the stone.

Lord Cai arose, unsteady with the mead in his belly and head, and roared out the great news that Excalibur had been freed from the stone. He held up Arthur's arm so that the sword tip pointed to the heavens, while the besotted lords slowly absorbed the news. They began their usual snarling and growling, furious that the young squire had achieved the result they had each so ardently sought. But Lord Ulfius was able to quell the disorder by announcing that they would test the young squire the next morning, to confirm the truth of the curious event.

In the courtyard behind the Pilsdon church Ulfius thrust the sword back into the stone. Then, keenly observed by the assembly of lords, Arthur grasped the hilt and pulled Excalibur out of its strange resting place. The lords made no secret of their dismay and disgust. But only I knew the secret of Merlin's device, and that Merlin must have taught Arthur how to release Excalibur.

✧

The lords, their wives and ladies-in--waiting, squires, cooks, armorers, carpenters, midwives, children, farmers and their families were called to appear in the great courtyard in front of Cadbury Castle to hail the young man, Arthur, who was to be named king of Britain on the following day. Because of my station in the court I stood at Merlin's side, in the group near Arthur. It was the first time that I was able to observe Arthur at close hand.

Although he had passed only seventeen winters, he was already taller than many of the lords. His frame was slender and he moved with remarkable ease, like a great cat. Like our mother, Ygraine, his hair was blond. His eyes, like hers, were intensely blue and piercing. He smiled when I was presented to him and he expressed his gratitude for the comforts of his new status at the castle. He spoke clearly and calmly, with a pleasing, bell-like tone. His manner was modest and suggested a true interest in my responses.

I told him that he was about to be declared my king, and that his comfort would be my overriding concern for as long as I was responsible for the management of the castle's household affairs. He looked at me quietly, smiled, and thanked me.

☼

Despite Merlin's resistance, the bishop emerged the victor in their argument over the site for Arthur's coronation. The bishop insisted that the ceremony be held in the new chapel at Cadbury castle. Merlin later told me that it was a small compromise to make in return for the bishop's agreement to keep the secret of Arthur's rearing by Lord Auctor.

When I asked Merlin about this compromise with the Christian faith, he looked at me sidelong and said that there were many things I was not to fear, that our Druid gods and goddesses would always be more powerful than the one god of the Christian belief.

✿

The bishop had been conducting regular instruction of the children of the court in the Christian faith. Now his new chapel at Cadbury Castle would become a consecrated place because it would shelter the coronation of the first Christian king of Britain.

The chapel was small. Only the older lords and knights and their ladies were in attendance. I sat at Merlin's side during the ceremony. I had never witnessed so solemn and vivid a display of colors and power. These men were ready to swear to serve their king to the death, if need be.

The bishop invoked the blessings of God, a Holy Ghost, and Jesus Christ, asking them to look benevolently on the acts of the man who was about to become Britain's new king. He asked Arthur to swear, in the name of God, to defend the Christian faith in all his acts as King of Britain.

In his high, ringing voice, Arthur did so swear. The bishop placed a crown of gold filigree on Arthur's head, and we stood to greet our king. We solemnly repeated, "Hail! Hail! Hail!" Then

the bishop asked us to kneel in our places while
he mumbled some long Latin sentences.

Arthur, king of Britain, had been confirmed as the new Pendragon. Now the angry
lords were to be united again.

☼

Each day of the week following the coronation ceremony Arthur and the assembly of lords
held councils to plan for the defence against our
enemies, the Saxons, Irish, and Picts. The household staff worked from daybreak to midnight
supplying food and drink. I remember our efforts
with some pride. As usual, Lady Ceinwen was
keenly alert to the needs of the lords, their wives,
and children, while she also made sure that our
household staff was properly cared for.

Arthur had asked four of the greater
landholder lords to remain at Cadbury to observe
the training of our warriors in horsemanship,
archery, and the lance and sword. I watched
those exercises with an eagerness I had never
before experienced.

It was clear to everyone that, despite his
youth, Arthur was already a master and a superb
teacher of the arts of war. The knights and
warriors of our little army at Cadbury were eager
for his instruction. They were exhilarated by his
attention, his constant encouragement, and by his

stern, calculated expectations. It was unlike anything I had seen during Uther's time.

☼

A few days after the lords had departed Arthur invited me to ride with him early one morning. Walking to the stables in that grey daybreak I saw the sky heavy with rolling clouds. But the mist that bathed the castle, the little village, and the surrounding fields and forests, all made me sweet with the feeling that I was walking through a very thin cloud that would lift me into sunlight again.

When I came to the stables I saw that Arthur was examining Wyn, his magnificent, nervous white stallion, while Erec held the reins. Erec was now the stable master. Arthur smiled at me and took Wyn's reins while Erec went to fetch my horse, Mabon. When I came closer and greeted him Arthur gazed directly into my eyes and said, simply, "Good morning, Lady Morgain. A lovely morning, indeed!"

I thanked Erec for bringing me my mare, Mabon. But he avoided my eyes and mumbled a polite reply. As I stepped on Erec's outstretched hand to mount I knew the familiar twinge of sadness for his plight.

Arthur told me to precede him in whatever direction I chose as we trotted away from the

Cadbury stables. I remember being amused by the sound of Wyn's insistent snorting and whinnying behind me. Wyn was accustomed to leadership among horses.

Then I realized that Arthur was not being merely polite in asking me to precede him. Riding close behind me he would be able to observe my ability on horse. That recognition pleased me and I urged Mabon into a fine canter. Now Wyn was distracted from his snortings and I could attend to the old, splendid pleasure of riding. Arthur kept Wyn at a precisely matched pace, close behind my Mabon. I was transported, happy, moving with Mabon's rhythm, taking her heat into my thighs, breathing the odors of wet earth and grasses, and the delicious, cool, wet air of the mist.

I had chosen the path to the forest beyond the meadows, the forest where Merlin and I had enjoyed each other, where I now hoped to enjoy Arthur. My horse's movement under me warmed my thighs while Arthur continued to ride close behind. When we came to the edge of the forest we dismounted to avoid the low branches and walked into the dark grey half-light under the wet trees. Arthur strode beside me, quiet, with a faint smile. We heard the water dripping from the boughs, the soft rustle of twigs and leaves, and the cush of our boots in the wet earth as we approached my secret clearing.

Standing in the clearing's center, I felt that Arthur and I were in an enchantment. But the brief spell was broken when Arthur addressed me.

He asked about my life at Cadbury before he came to it, while he opened a leather pouch that held some meat, bread, and a flask of mead. The ground was now fairly soaked, so we ate standing side by side at the trunk of a great oak.

I answered his questions as well as I could without revealing what I knew of his origin. Then he asked me to tell him what I had observed about Uther Pendragon, about Uther's qualities as a sovereign and judge, about his attitudes toward his liege lords, and about the circumstances of his death.

I answered all of his cleanly formed questions directly. When I briefly mentioned Merlin's position as Uther's advisor, I could see a fleeting change in Arthur's expression. But he continued to listen until I had answered his other questions, and then looked directly into my eyes.

"And Merlin?"

I told him, bluntly, that Merlin would become his most trusted ally, his friend, and his wisest councillor, if Arthur so wished. I went on to tell of Merlin's astounding knowledge, of his solitude, of his compassionate discretion. I felt, all the while I spoke, that Arthur was absorbing my words as completely as the ground beneath us drank the water drizzling from the sky above us. The mist was not lifting as I had hoped it would. Indeed, it had begun to rain softly.

Arthur thanked me for my answers and said that we had better return to the castle. As we came out of the forest to the edge of the meadow there was a sudden, tearing noise of lightning and the deep, threatening roll of thunder. Arthur held his hand to help me mount, then turned and leaped astride his stallion. We tied the hoods of our riding cloaks tight and galloped across the rainswept meadows to the Cadbury stables. Arthur, soaked, smiled and thanked me for my company and our conversation. I thanked him in turn, hardly able to see him clearly in the drenching rainfall.

Immediately after Erec had taken Mabon's reins I went to my chambers. I was deeply chilled and could not control my chattering teeth. Lady Ceinwen came to my room and helped me to remove my wet clothing. She made me lie on a sheepskin and rubbed me dry and warm with a coarse cloth.

Dear Ceinwen! You may remember that I told you that I had ridden with Arthur that morning. But I could not tell you then of my disappointment, that I had wished for much more than his questions about Cadbury and Uther. Before I fell asleep I wondered if the rain, the lightning, and the thunder were signs from my gods and goddesses. I slept heavily, without dreams.

✿

Three months after his coronation Arthur was put to his first trial as the warrior-leader of all the Britons. Our spies brought information that the Picts and the Irish planned to invade north and west Britain, in league with the Saxons invading from the south. We had never before been threatened by all three of our enemies at the same time.

Arthur ordered an assembly of all the people of Cadbury on the day after our spies had reported the enemies' preparation to invade us.

Standing on a high platform above the great crowd, he declared that we were about to suffer the last of all the despicable raids by the greedy Picts and Saxons. The crowd interrupted him with shouts of support and vile curses on the enemy. Arthur demanded silence, and then he cautioned that every person in his domain would be responsible for defending the castle and its lands.

He commanded the intensification of the training of all the men in the skills of defense, offense, and rout. All the women were to prepare foods for the warriors. Those who remained at the castle were to collect and wash cloths for bandages, to gather and prepare the herbs, roots, and berries needed for medicines, and to convert the great hall into a hospital for treating our wounded.

He ordered the knights, squires, and foot soldiers to bring their weapons to the armorers for sharpening, to make every cutting and thrusting blade inflict the severest, mortal if possible, wounds on the enemy. The lords were to begin daily, concentrated training of their knights and foot soldiers in horsemanship, archery, and the wielding of swords and lances, following the instructions Arthur had been teaching during the last three months.

Then, in his ringing voice, he shouted, "These raids will end at their beginnings! We Britons will be victorious! Victory! Victory!"

The crowd echoed his call to victory in a great, single voice. I had never heard so powerful a speech before from any of the leaders, including Uther himself. Arthur's body and spirit filled his words and made them blaze in our minds as we listened. We went to our duties marvelously light in heart.

For the rest of that day his face, his voice, and his body burned in a frightening but thrilling way in my memory. In my room that night I imagined enjoying him for a long time. I could not fall asleep until the sky began to change color with the rising sun.

☼

Immediately after his coronation Arthur had named Lord Cai seneschal of the court. Cai's good humor was felt by all who served him, and now we were able to observe how good and intelligent a man he was. He had offered to accompany Arthur on the expedition against our enemies, but Arthur insisted that Cai remain at Cadbury, to prepare the castle to become a last stronghold if need be. A small armed force, consisting mainly of older men and young lads, was mustered for the castle's defense. Cai drilled them mercilessly and humorously, and behaved in the same manner as he went about managing the women's and children's tasks.

I had the responsibility of preparing the great hall to serve as a hospital. Fifty pallets were laid out, and I trained six young women to care for our wounded.

During the four days of that war I spent some time at my quicksilver mirror. Arthur was the most daring and violent of all the violent and daring men he led. He had taken command of the group that was to resist the Saxons at the shoreline near Chysauster. He kept his men and their horses hidden behind rocks and in the depressions of sand dunes. Just as our spies had told us, the greedy Saxons approached the beach in their longships and prepared to land under cover of the heavy fog that blanketed the shore.

Arthur waited until most of the Saxon warriors had jumped into the shallow water and were trudging up to dry land. He raised Excalibur high above his head, and our warriors roared terrifying, barking sounds as they raced through the swirling mists toward the bewildered Saxons. The Saxons could only retreat back into the water. They were cut down and then hacked like fallen animals.

Our archers shot flame-arrows that kindled raging fires in two of the longships. The Saxon survivors, confused and angry at having been trapped like wild pigs, sailed away to the south.

Our force lost only a few men in that battle. Arthur led his men to camp on a bluff overlooking the shore; but the Saxons did not return. The following day Arthur and his men joined with the forces that were to resist the Picts north of Meare. Lord Ulfius, who was in command there, had repelled their probing sorties and was now waiting to face their attack.

The invaders could not hold against our cavalry and archers, and they retreated in rout. No wounded or fallen men were allowed to survive, for we had learned long ago that making prisoners of our enemies sapped our own food stores. I watched as Arthur and Ulfius, standing in the meadow strewn with slaughtered warriors and horses, embraced each other, exulting in their victory. I turned away from my mirror, retching in nausea and disgust.

Later that night I imagined making Arthur my prisoner, alive in my bed. But in my dreams he became my master, and I his slave.

✡

I knew that Merlin would surely return to the castle in time to care for our wounded men, but I did not know when. I knew that his seeing gift would alert him, and it did. He arrived at the castle on the day before our warriors returned. He inspected my preparations in the hospital, and then he turned to me and said that it would be a source of great happiness to him if all these efforts became unnecessary. After a pause, he looked sharply at me and said, "But that will never be, will it?"

✿

I could hear the heavy noises of horses and wagons. I ran to my window slit to see our warriors approaching the castle, victorious. Arthur, at the spearhead, sang with the men in praise of the one god, and the gods and the goddesses, for not all the men were converted to the Christian faith. I made my silent thanks to my own goddesses, who had protected Arthur.

✿

We had very few wounded to care for, so the great hall was cleared of the pallet beds to prepare for the victory feast that Arthur had ordered immediately after he dismounted.

Barrels of mead were rolled into the great hall, and the smells of roasting meats and baking bread quickly changed the flavors of the air in the castle. Long tables were set on the courtyard to feed the foot soldiers, archers, and armorers.

The mead barrels were opened and decanted. I had decided some time before that I would not drink mead or other wines because I did not like their effect on my thinking and movement. But on this occasion I did sip once from Lord Cai's cup when we arose to hail Arthur, our king, on his great victory. Arthur was flushed with happiness and the many cups he had already drained.

☼

Dear Ceinwen! What I am about to say may shock you. Please write all this down. Don't stop!

You may have suspected, but I doubt that you know what happened on the night of Arthur's first victory feast. We have reached that time in our lives when the past becomes dimmer, and when we ourselves shall be passing over, as Arthur has. The past will change only in the way we remember it. But I do remember everything as it happened. Bear with me, Ceinwen.

☼

At the feast in the castle after Arthur's great victory I watched him, glowing with his success, grow more and more dulled and lax with the mead in his belly and brain. Merlin sat close to him and helped him to sit erect in his king's chair. I saw Arthur losing his wonderful, high manner. I felt anguish and turned away to watch the jugglers walking among the tables.

A boy, about eight or nine years old, delighted us by taking an apple and a pear from a bowl on our table to toss them into the air, one after the other, in his right hand.

He held his left hand high and pointed his forefinger, like the tip of a sword, to the roof of the hall. I watched his intense, lovely face and his black eyes fixed on the two fruits he floated from his hand. There was a tight smile on his lips. In that brief span of time his world was an apple and a pear.

I excused myself from the group of lords and their ladies and left the hall. There were no guards in front of Arthur's bedroom, and I knew the feast and the draughts of mead had relaxed all of them into stupor, anyway. I went into Arthur's bedchamber.

I hid myself among the robes that were hanging behind the thick, heavy tapestry. I stepped out of my smallclothes and put them under my breasts. Then I tied my belt around my waist again. Now I would be ready to enjoy Arthur.

The robes that hid me smelled of fur, flax, and wool. I could faintly identify Arthur's sweat. It made me quiver with the excitement of what I intended to do, to do what my dreams had been unfolding.

When Arthur's bedchamber door opened I saw that Merlin was helping him walk to his bed. Arthur was besotted. Merlin stripped our king of all his clothes and covered him with a heavy sheepskin. Then Merlin glanced around the dimly lit room and went away.

I waited for a while before I moved out of my hiding place and into Arthur's bed. The smell of Arthur's sweat was spiced with the mead he had drunk. I softly stroked his chest and moved my hand down to his cok. I cupped him and heard Arthur moan in his sleep. I held his cok softly until it grew long and firm. I pulled my skirt above my belly and straddled his groin. I was now raging with desire and I could feel that glorious moistening, itching, and burning in the fork of my thighs. My heat stiffened Arthur's cok even more, and I enclosed myself on it.

Arthur moaned again, this time in pleasure. I know that sound well. But he remained asleep while I moved easily and slowly up and down. After a few caressing strokes I felt the snap and flood of his spurting fill me. I sat quietly astride him for a while, resisting my own wish for enjoyment in my fear of awakening him. Then I carefully uncoupled from him and left his bed.

I quickly stemmed the drip of his juice by making a diaper of my smallclothes, pressing the cloth into my cunnus. Then I tied the belt around my dress again to hold the diaper in place. I would, I must, conceive a son by Arthur.

As I stepped out of Arthur's bedchamber a hand suddenly gripped my wrist. Startled, I turned to see Merlin. He whispered that I must never again enter Arthur's room, that I should remember that Arthur was my half-brother. I fixed my gaze into his silvery eyes and knew that he would never be able to hurt me. He loved me, in his way. I said nothing. I loosened his grip on my wrist and walked down the corridor to my own bedroom.

✪

On the afternoon of the day after our child was conceived I asked Arthur for an audience. He was surprised at my use of that word. He smiled and asked me to speak my mind. I said that he of course knew that I was a noblewoman of the highest rank, the daughter of Ygraine and Gorlois, and the stepdaughter of Uther Pendragon, Arthur's predecessor. I said that, as Arthur was unmarried, and because I was six years older than he, I deserved to share in the responsibilities of governing.

Arthur listened quietly. His smile faded. He asked whether I was dissatisfied with my present duties as mistress of the household affairs, if I found Lord Cai at odds with my management of the women's work. I replied that I had always found household affairs dull, that I had an understanding of the relations between Britain and Rome, that I was well educated in the Druid beliefs, and finally, that I could attend to the care of the women and children of Cadbury.

Arthur was silent for some time after I had spoken. Then he said that he wished me to continue my status as mistress of the household of Cadbury Castle, and expressed his gratitude for all that I had already done.

I thought about his reply and then asked for permission to visit my step-sister, Morgause, and her husband King Loth in Orkney. Arthur replied warmly, offering whatever I might need to make my voyage as comfortable as possible.

I knew now that Arthur would never share his power with me, and that despite his smiles and warmth, he was afraid of me.

☼

You will remember, dear Ceinwen, how I moved to Orkney a few days after that splendid victory feast. And you will remember how I grew larger with the child I carried. You never asked the name of his father. I would not have told you if you had.

Now I can tell you that my child was Mordred, who lies in his grave at Camlann. I could not prevent his path from cutting so deeply and fatally into Arthur's.

☼

Morgause, my step-sister, had married King Loth seven years after I moved with my mother to Uther's Cadbury Castle. Morgause and her husband were deeply fond of each other, and Loth trusted her counsel in all matters. Morgause was even more beautiful than I remembered her. Now she was matronly, with the lightness of walk and carriage that comes with good health and constant happiness in the marriage bed. Three splendid sons, Gawain, Ewain, and Gaharis, held the highest places in their parents' esteem and concern. I do not think I could have chosen a better place to await my birthing trial.

Loth was one of those men who loves the world and all its wonders. I had at first thought that Morgause might not be happy in a marriage with a husband who was, at the time of their wedding, almost twice her age. But he showed his constant love for her every day, she told me, and the peace and beauty of his farmlands were always secondary to his esteem for his family.

He behaved toward me with respect and concern for my situation as a noblewoman who was to bring a bastard into the world. But he never pressed me to tell the name of the child's father, and he had instructed everyone in his household to respect my wish to be undisturbed.

Morgause and Loth had agreed to raise my child as their own, and so dispelled any fear that remained in my spirit about what I was doing.

In my pregnancy I became aware of feelings I had never known. I had not felt anxiety ever since the death of my mother. I knew the need to be more careful about my body. So I did not ride during all those beautiful months while my child was growing inside me.

Morgause found a good woman to be my midwife. Her name was Meriel, and she had mothered children of her own. She was born and raised on one of the farms in Loth's realm, and her children were now farmers and the wives of farmers. I could just barely understand her language at first. We spoke to each other by gestures, smiles, and frowns. But Morgause had learned the language of the Orkneys and when necessary she became our interpreter.

☼

As Uther's daughter by Heulwen, his second wife, Morgause was kin to Arthur, but I never spoke of that to her. Morgause and I talked about the strange circumstances of Arthur's assumption to the throne of Britain. Unlike me, Morgause had no wish for status in Arthur's court, nor could she imagine herself a governing figure among those violent, selfish lords. She was happy to be Loth's wife, to care for him and their sons.

I did not tell her of my maddening desire to share power with Arthur. I had never been able to erase the memory of how he was conceived by Uther's forced enjoyment of my mother, nor could I forget that Uther had butchered my father. Those memories visited me often and troubled my sleep throughout the time of my pregnancy. But I never told Morgause what I had seen Uther do to my mother.

✡

Taw, my raven, had become my single, devoted pet. I trimmed his damaged wing so that it no longer dragged so pitifully on the ground. I did not like him to walk too closely behind me, as he did for a few months after I rescued him. Now he observed my caution to stay three paces behind me when I walked. He stopped in place when I stopped, and he waited until I flicked my fingers to signal him to follow me or to come closer.

His voice was now less harsh and raucous. I spoke simply to him, as though I were addressing a child. I would look directly into his odd, amber eyes when I spoke to him. They were the only features of his ferocious face that responded with understanding, thinking, and pleasure when

I stroked the top of his head, and with anger when I scolded him.

When I scolded him the color of his eyes changed. I could see a red glow forming under the amber. I always stroked his head after such an event, and I remember my amazement, the first time, at the gradual change to amber again. Red, then, was the inner color of his controlled anger, as it so often is in men and women.

Taw sat with me in my room at Loth's castle while I said silent prayers to my priestesses and developed my skills in making medicines. I tried to use my quicksilver mirror. But I was unable to summon images from the past, nor to be transported to other places in the present. After some nights of staring into the quicksilver without success I thought that perhaps my pregnancy interfered with my magic. In my pregnancy, I, Morgain, had perhaps become a vessel of the past, the present, and the future. So I set aside the bowl of quicksilver and lived quietly and serenely until my birthing trial would come.

☼

Loth and Morgause enjoyed games with their children, and Roman Mill was one of the games we played one evening each week. Loth had placed markers and lines on the floor of the hall of the castle, and our game pieces were nine boys and girls, children from the court and nearby farms.

You know that game, Ceinwen. It was amusing and lifted me from the growing sluggishness of my body. Dear Morgause was especially skillful and would be the winner more often than I. But I learned to observe her eyes as she studied the developing situation on the floor. The children became impatient while waiting for Morgause's instruction to move, and their chatter and giggling distracted her. I found that my attention to her eyes gave me clues to her moves and the time to plan my counter moves.

One night, a few weeks after the winter solstice, the game was interrupted by the onset of my birthing trial. I was helped to the room Morgause had prepared for that event, and Meriel, my midwife, became my physician, my nurse, and my friend.

I had prepared myself for bearing the pains I had witnessed during the birthing trials of other women. With the help of one of my potions I placed myself in trance.

☿

My child, a boy, came out of me as the sun arose next morning over the white, snow-blanketed world. His cries were sweet sounds to me. But when Meriel placed him in my arms to nurse, a quiver shook my body. I saw the red smear of the scarlet birthmark on his neck and cheek.

I put him to my breast and turned to look at Meriel. My question must have leaped from my eyes to hers.

Meriel moved to the foot of my bed. She nodded slowly and said,

"You know, Lady, I have never asked you to tell me of this little one's conception. I have helped you to remain strong and to prepare for this moment, all through these wonderful months. But when your baby came into the air I could see that he was made in a sinful act.

"Forgive me, dear Lady, you know that I am a simple woman. But the mark on his cheek will be hateful to him for as long as he lives, and so he is destined to serve the Darkness. He will not bring light into this world, and so he should not be allowed to grow in this world. If you wish, I will take him away and . . ."

I screamed at Meriel and told her to leave the room. She sobbed as she turned away. Then I watched my baby suckle and I thanked my gods and goddesses for their gift.

Morgause's Druid came late in the afternoon for the naming ceremony. My son was given the name I had fixed in my mind on the night of his conception, Mordred.

✿

In the springtime of Mordred's first year we were commanded by Lord Cai to attend the wedding ceremony of Arthur and Guinevere at Cadbury. Loth remembered Guinevere as the daughter of another liege lord, Lodegrance, a Christian.

I had tried to accustom myself to the inevitable separation from my little boy, but daily I faced the shock of loving in a way I had never known before. My son! I cannot describe that loving.

Morgause had selected a young village woman to be his wet nurse. I watched him greedily sucking at her breast and called on my gods and goddesses to protect him.

Morgause, Loth, and I set out on the voyage to Cadbury on that calm day, the day when Mordred reached his fourth month. I was not to see him again for four years.

✿

Arthur was the youngest of the fractious kings and lords who squabbled over their rights in the forging of what they called a unified Britain. Merlin told me that Arthur had decided that, with a queen beside him, he would command greater authority over the liege lords. His choice, Guinevere, was the daughter of a friendly king, Lodegrance. Arthur had met Guinevere during a visit to Lodegrance's castle at Camarthen.

I learned from Merlin that Lodegrance's lands and castle controlled the northern marshlands, a natural barrier against the ferocious, raiding Picts. Guinevere would inherit her father's lands, and the marriage would give Arthur another stronghold in the defense of Britain. The wedding ceremony would take place on the day after the spring equinox.

☼

It was the custom to invite wedding parties to stay at Cadbury Castle for a few weeks before the ceremony, so that the bishop could instruct the betrothed couple in the Christian rules of marriage. But Guinevere and her party did not arrive until the very day of the ceremony.

Merlin's expression was unusually sombre and downcast as he told me that Guinevere had already been instructed at Camarthen, since Lodegrance had become a Christian a few years before. I could see that he was deeply troubled by the growing power of the new, Roman Christian teachings.

☼

On the wedding day the great hall of Cadbury Castle held about a hundred people, men, women, and children in wonderfully colored clothes. I have always delighted in the colors of birds, trees, and flowers that are seen at wedding ceremonies. The guests chattered and murmured, rather like a congress of birds, awaiting the arrival of Guinevere's party.

Lodegrance had sent an impressive gift to Arthur, a huge, round table capable of seating many people comfortably. It was wonderfully made of oak, with a carved design of intertwined twigs, leaves, and acorns around its rim. It filled one corner of the great hall.

I sat on the raised platform with Lady Ceinwen. At my other side, Merlin, Arthur, and the bishop quietly whispered to each other while we waited. We heard the approaching sounds of horses, drums, and raucous ram-horns. When the doors of the great hall were opened the wild sounds filled and echoed in the hall.

Guinevere dismounted and entered at the head of her family and their knights. Guinevere and the rest must have stopped earlier that morning, to refresh themselves and change their clothes at some place not too distant. They showed no sign of dust or fatigue from their long journey.

The hall was crowded with Lodegrance's knights and their squires, all young men, and Guinevere's ladies-in-waiting. They had been promised by Lodegrance as his wedding gift to

Arthur, in friendship and support for Arthur's aims.

My first impression as she walked toward our platform was that Guinevere had been formed by sunlight itself. Her hair was of a golden, ripe flax color. As she came closer I saw that two braids had been fastened at their ends, above her forehead, by a device made of a violet-colored stone. When I saw the violet color of her eyes, I thought for a moment that she had been gifted with a third eye. It was of course not so, but I was momentarily shaken by my mind's flight. Guinevere had arranged her hair to form a crown, before being declared a queen.

She continued her flowing gait until she reached our platform, her gaze now fixed on Arthur's glowing face. Arthur stepped down to take his place at her side. I watched the two shining figures keenly while the bishop arose to stand at the center of the platform. Dressed in his pure white gown, decorated only by the bright red cross on its front, the bishop was the dominant figure in the great hall.

Guinevere was tall, the top of her head at the height of Arthur's eyes. For just a few moments she turned to look at me, and I smiled. But she made no visible sign of greeting. She looked at me but did not see me.

In his heavy, droning voice the bishop greeted and blessed the assembly. Then he began to intone the Christian marriage litany, holding his hands above the heads of Arthur and Guinevere. As they listened I again felt the click of my mind's inward eye.

I undressed Guinevere. Under the gold-colored, filigree cloth of her gown I saw her pear-shaped breasts with their upturned points. My gaze moved down her slender, firm waist to her hips, too narrow for easy birthing, but her mound was high and soft. Her legs were smooth and lightly muscled. The thought that she had indeed been formed for enjoyment was oddly thrilling.

I saw Arthur, golden in the torchlight of their bedchamber, as he mouthed her breasts and navel. Then I remembered the absence of such pleasure when I straddled Arthur, half asleep, besotted and vague, to conceive my son.

My inward images dissolved as I heard the bishop's droning voice ask Arthur and Guinevere to repeat the marriage vows. Arthur accepted Guinevere as his wife until death would part them, and then Guinevere repeated her vows in almost a whisper, as if she were talking in her sleep. The bishop raised his voice to declare them man and wife in the eyes of God, and the great hall resounded with shouts of good wishes.

Arthur turned to the assembly and raised his hand for quiet, smiling as he did so. In his brilliant, ringing voice he declared that, to celebrate this day, he would form a fellowship of Knights of the Round Table, fifty of the purest and bravest knights in all Britain. These men were to be the models for all the lordly rulers of a united Britain, by their purity, their allegiance, and their readiness to give their lives in the great cause of unifying Britain. The assembly was silent for a few moments, then roared, "King Arthur, hail King Arthur!" and stamped their feet in unison.

✿

As I tell this to you, Ceinwen, as you write down my words, I can see your faint, rueful smile. You and I have seen and heard so many men make such stirring speeches, with their promises rising like the gases over the marshlands.

✿

Guiomar, Guinevere's brother, was among the knights that Lodegrance had brought to enter Arthur's company of warriors. Guiomar was four or five years older than his sister. He was courteously presented to me by his father during the feast that followed the wedding ceremony.

Lodegrance explained to Guiomar the position I held in the court. How, as Ygraine's daughter and Uther's stepdaughter, I was the lady responsible for the housekeeping and hospitalling in Cadbury Castle. Now Guinevere, as queen, would assume those responsibilities.

Guiomar's gaze locked with mine as we listened to Lodegrance's kindly, respectful explanation. Then Lodegrance left us to join his friends elsewhere in the great hall. Guiomar courteously asked Lady Ceinwen to move from her seat so that he could sit beside me. Guiomar's eyes--intensely blue, like Arthur's--fixed me in a way that can be understood only by those who have experienced the spontaneous, mutual heat of desire's flame.

In the noisy disorder of the feast it was quite easy for us to leave the hall, separately as we had tremblingly agreed, to meet near the stables. When I came there Guiomar was waiting for me. He held his hands outstretched to me. I clasped them in mine and he drew me to him to press me against his body. As I looked up into his face I could see the evening stars glistening around his head.

With that first kiss I was taken, for the first time in my life as a woman, into a different, miraculous abode of love. I cannot describe the sharings, the gifts, and the abandon of that night.

After our first enjoyment in the meadow we walked on to the enchanted crystal pond of Merlin's quarry.

In that pure water we swam and loved again under the Moon surrounded by her friends, the stars.

From that night onward Guiomar and I met secretly, every night. It is one thing to tell of loving, and quite another to know it.

✿

Our secret enjoyment seemed limitless until one day I was summoned to Arthur's small council chamber. I was surprised and forewarned by the presence of Guinevere, who sat at Arthur's side. Guiomar stood before them with his head bowed.

Remorse? Secret defiance? I was not immediately sure.

As soon as I had reached the place at Guiomar's side Guinevere began to speak to me in low, bitter tones. She said that our secret meetings had been reported to Arthur and herself, that we were disgracing the court, and that--and here she turned to Arthur with an apologetic smile--she considered me the lecherous debaucher of a pure knight. She stared at Guiomar and coldly told him that he had brought dishonor to their father, and to Arthur's court.

Then she turned to Arthur and asked that he banish me from Cadbury.

Arthur raised his eyes to look at me. He studied me silently for a few moments before he expressed his approval of Guinevere's request. I understood immediately that they had made that decision well before I had been summoned to them.

He said that it was impossible for him to allow such behavior among the knights and ladies in his court, which he was determined to establish as a model of honor and dedication.

He said that he wished me to return to Tintagel, my childhood home. He would provide me with guards and the necessities for a small company of knights and for my ladies and servants, until we could arrange to care for ourselves. The banishment was to be in force immediately.

Guiomar spoke not a word in the silence that followed. I had hoped that he would at least declare his love for me and his certainty of my love for him. I observed him. He said nothing.

I did not smile. I felt no tears welling in my eyes. My king and queen had made a decision that I knew was unchangeable. And I knew that Guinevere had become my enemy, and that

Arthur would do nothing to persuade her to accept my rightful place in his court, or in his life.

I knew, too, that any expression of anger or protest would give Arthur and Guinevere the license to demean me further, and probably make the terms of my banishment more severe. They were Christians. I had never accepted the new faith. I remain a Druid.

Indeed, I felt a welcome release from my responsibilities as the first lady in Arthur's service, for that is what it was. I turned away from them and walked out of the chamber.

✡

Guiomar! How I loved him, and still do! How we loved each other and whispered our dreams of a life together!

Now, although Guiomar would be trained as a warrior knight, his wish to enter the fellowship of the Round Table would never be realized. He was no longer "pure."

The ladies of the court would chatter among themselves, some of them envious of our loving. But such chatter was of no consequence in courtly matters. They would chatter, and in the main admire Guinevere for her decision, for it surely must have been hers. And too, they would live somewhat more at ease in my absence.

✡

We left Cadbury Castle three days later. A few workmen bowed respectfully to us as our small company of knights, artisans and servants approached the gates. Then, in breathtaking freedom, we cantered over meadows and gentle forests that lay between us and Tintagel.

I was flooded with delight at seeing my childhood home again. Tintagel was in a mist of ocean spume. We rested and watched the brilliant double rainbow that glowed in the eastern sky, a sign from my gods and goddesses.

Our little company dismounted in front of Tintagel's gate. Only you, Ceinwen, and I had known this place before that day.

I talked to my company about my father's reign and the many raids the fortress had repelled. I felt such a deep happiness as I entered the great hall and moved through those well-remembered rooms, the kitchen, the ladies' weaving and sewing rooms. So many sweet memories!

Then I went to my own bedchamber. At the far wall my parents' bedchamber door was slightly ajar. I walked cautiously to look into the room. Everything was clean, undisturbed, waiting. The heavy sheepskin on my parents' bed glistened in a ray of sunlight. I suddenly felt faint and ill.

☼

You will remember, Ceinwen, how you helped me to my bed and cared for me during those days. You were kind, but really helpless. It was during that time that I could tell you, at last, what I knew about Uther's deception and rape of my mother. I knew that I must talk to you to dispel the demons that danced in my brain. You were so calm then, as you are even now.

☆

I remained in that feeble, troubled state for several days. I thought so often of Mordred, my son, wishing him to be with me at Tintagel. And then of the danger to him if his presence became known to Arthur and Guinevere. How could I explain his very existence? So I resigned myself to his rearing by Morgause and Loth.

We had been at Tintagel for about a month when we received a visit from Merlin. He came to tell me that Arthur had decided that I must marry and that my husband was to be Lord Uryens, the ruler of Gorlot, a large landhold in the north. Merlin said that Uryens was another strong warrior leader, and that he was at least twice my age at the time.

I asked Merlin how he could be a party to such a decision. He replied simply that Arthur was his king, that Arthur's wishes were to be obeyed, and that I was to prepare for the wedding that was to take place as soon as I could return to Cadbury Castle, where Lord Uryens awaited me.

A furious, murderous knot in my stomach made me turn away from Merlin. I did not look at him when I replied that I would arrive at Cadbury within two days. I walked away and went to my workroom.

I called Taw to my side. I spoke quietly to him, asking that he help me punish Arthur for his insult to my spirit and body.

Taw listened, then cocked his head to one side. I stroked his neck and head as I sat, thinking. There could be only two reasons for Arthur's imperious decision that I marry Lord Uryens.

The first must be that the marriage was devised to seal a pact to make Uryens liege to Arthur. The second must be to keep me at a great distance from Cadbury Castle.

I had become a thorn in Arthur's larger schemes, and I well knew how I was regarded by Guinevere. I had no alternative but to obey.

☼

Upon my arrival at Cadbury Castle I was escorted to the council chamber. Arthur and Guinevere welcomed me and introduced me to my future husband, Lord Uryens. He was indeed a huge man, a Scot, his golden blond hair and beard streaked with grey. His smile was honest and warm, and I sensed that he would try to be a gentle husband.

I was polite but cool with Arthur and Guinevere, and they treated me similarly. They thanked me for responding so swiftly to their request. Their behavior simply confirmed my thought that there were considerations other than my welfare underlying my marriage to Uryens. So I decided to behave obediently to my king, and to appear to be chastened by my fall from his grace.

With Uryens, as we walked in one of the gardens, I was both austere and gracious. I suggested that his will would be my own if I found no reason to behave in another fashion and that, as my husband, his comfort would be my overriding concern.

He replied that he had observed me with great pleasure when he had attended the wedding ceremony of Arthur and Guinevere, and that he was deeply happy that I had accepted his and their wish that I marry him.

☼

My wedding gown was being made by Cardywyn, the dressmaker at Cadbury, and she asked me to come for a fitting later that afternoon. I used that waiting time well. To advance my revenge against Arthur and Guinevere I sent word to Erec to visit me in my chamber. Erec had been made the senior squire and now served Arthur himself.

Erec glowed with pleasure at seeing me again. He was proud to have become Arthur's squire, and very handsome, moving in that lithe way of men who are bonded to horses. Like horses, such men seem to think with their muscles. He was no longer the scruffy stable boy.

I greeted him with a brief, light kiss on his cheek and felt his responsive quiver. I told him of my need for several squires to become spies who would help me to annoy and humiliate Arthur and his knights. Erec stepped away. He said he was frightened of such a dangerous adventure. I moved to him, clasped his waist and pressed my bosom and hips close to his fine body. He shivered, and agreed to help me.

My plan was simple. Squires always accompanied their knights when they went hunting, when they visited farmers to collect taxes, and whenever they rode in defense of our lands against raiders. Away from the castle, the squires prepared the meals for their knights. I planned to affect the knights' behavior with my trance-making potions. I had tested them with cats and dogs. Now I knew that I must try to use them with men. These were tools of the black magic that Merlin shunned. But I had become a prisoner of my own rage. I had no other choice.

I told Erec he would receive my instructions after my wedding ceremony. His face saddened. He nodded in helpless surrender to my plan.

☼

Only one unpleasant thing occurred during the preparation for the wedding ceremony. Arthur had asked the bishop to perform the marriage rite, without questioning me or Uryens about our wishes. I quietly said that I would not be married as a Christian, as I had never accepted that faith, and that I wished to be married under Druid custom by Merlin. Lord Uryens immediately affirmed his desire to accommodate me, as he was not devoted to any faith at all.

Arthur flushed with irritation at my resistance, but quickly calmed himself. He agreed to allow Merlin to perform the ceremony if I would agree to the bishop's blessing of the assembly before Merlin administered the rites. I agreed.

☼

The guests filled the great hall. Uryens and I, Arthur and Guinevere, the bishop and Merlin sat on the newly carved chairs that Uryens had brought as gifts to the court. I scanned the brilliant display of rainbow colors in the guests' plumages, dresses, and robes, and played my mind's game of recalling the names of birds whose colors I could see in the hall.

The bishop intoned his blessing and then Merlin arose to ask Uryens and me to stand before him. I listened but did not pay much attention to Merlin's almost whispered words. When Merlin asked us to face each other I had to tilt my head backward to look up into Uryens's eyes. He was indeed very tall. For just a moment I remembered my old fear of Uther Pendragon, and a quiet voice in my head asked if Arthur had indeed willed me to another brutish man.

But Uryens' eyes shone with happiness and the intensity of his desire for me. I smiled while I listened to Merlin's silvery, quiet voice. Again, I avoided Merlin's gaze. He finished the ceremony with a few more words.

At the wedding feast, in my new status as wife to a lord, I strolled among the tables to greet and thank the guests for their presence. I went to the long table set for the squires at the wall. Erec smiled and nodded, to indicate that he had begun to recruit squires for my plan.

I saw the black-haired boy juggler again and stopped to watch as, now using both hands, he tossed two apples and two pears, rising and falling. He smiled briefly at me. But he kept his attention fixed on his expanding world, now two apples, two pears.

Two singers among the musicians held my attention. One was a boy whose pure voice drew me into remembering the sweetness of my childhood, before my father's murder. The other was a young woman whose voice soared like a lark's in abandon and passion. I asked her name. It was Niniane. Then I asked if she would like to move to my court at Gorlot. She smiled and said she would like that. In our brief conversation I learned that she had never known her parents, and that she had been raised to serve as a milkmaid in one of Cadbury's farms. Later, Arthur graciously gave me permission to take her to Gorlot.

✡

Uryens and I retired to our marriage chamber very late that night. He had been careful not to make himself too drowsy with mead, and so we did enjoy each other for a while before we fell into a heavy sleep. I was a married woman. My husband was gentle, and utterly innocent of the manners of enjoyment.

✡

On the following morning I asked Erec to assemble the Cadbury squires to receive gifts from Uryens and me for their courtesy to our Gorlot knights. I told him to bring them to my room in small groups, and to be sure that one of those groups be composed only of those willing to aid in my plan. Uryens was in conference with Arthur, so I was able to talk with Erec's recruits privately.

I anticipated that the squires who would be most willing to become my spies would be those who served the more eminent knights of the court. Their eminence usually bred a grating arrogance that was expressed in the treatment of their squires. So some squires, intelligent, hard--working and hard-driven young men, would grow to resent, silently of course, the manners of their masters. I hoped they might be ready for my plan to humiliate their masters.

Erec was able to recruit five squires from among the hundred at Cadbury. I name them here, as this may be their only memorial. All have now passed on to the Other World, slaughtered in the horrible, inevitable wars to realize Arthur's vision:

Cemlyn, squire to Sir Alpin. Elfed, squire to Sir Dugald.

Gethin, squire to Sir Iwain. Gwilyun, squire to Sir Deinol.

And Emyr, squire to Sir Owain.

They know my gratitude.

☼

I knew that we would stay at Cadbury for a fortnight after our wedding, so I had prepared a device to be the first of my challenges to Arthur's status.

Usually all the nobles, their knights, and ladies gathered in the great hall for the midday feasts, for that is what those meals were indeed. Rivers of mead and many platters of lamb, vegetable dishes, and fruits were consumed every day. The mead continued to flow well after the meals had ended, and everyone softened under its influence.

Ever since my childhood at Tintagel I had kept a beautiful large horn, taken from a magnificent bull. It had been my father's favorite drinking horn because it could hold several long draughts. In my workroom I had been able to fix the horn in a certain way, and now, at Arthur's court, I was able to put it to use.

I instructed Niniane to bring the horn to Arthur and to explain that she had received it from a stranger outside the castle gate. I instructed her to tell Arthur that the stranger had warned her that the drinking horn could reveal whether or not a wife was enjoying any man other than her husband. If the mead spilled on his chest while he drank, then his wife was guilty of infidelity.

Niniane did well in this first test of her service to me. Arthur and the others at our table were immediately aroused. Arthur was already besotted, and declared that he must be the first to try the test. He called for a servant to fill the horn. When Arthur took his first draught, some drops of mead leaked out of the horn, wetting his tunic. I realized that I had made an error in the horn's secret design.

Arthur flew into a hissing rage. He grabbed a knife and threatened to stab Guinevere. But Iwain and Uryens were able to subdue him, urging him to think of the horn as an odd toy. Then Guinevere calmly offered to prove her innocence by the ordeal of fire. Arthur turned away from her and roughly ordered the other men at his table to take the test of the horn. Somehow, all except Uryens and Iwain stained themselves with mead.

Arthur, aware of Guinevere's discomfort and the embarrassment of the other ladies, recovered his good humor and sarcastically pronounced the horn a wonderful gift. He thanked Niniane and dismissed her. As soon as she moved away Arthur, again suddenly angry, turned and gave the horn to Sir Bleddyn and uttered a coarse remark that made Guinevere blush. She said nothing and sipped again from her cup. Merlin sat silently, observing us.

My first humiliation of Arthur was successful. I rejoiced secretly.

☼

Among the young knights who came with King Uryens to Cadbury Castle for my marriage ceremony was a Scot, Sir Accolon, Uryens' personal guard. He was very well made, just a bit taller than I, with raven black hair and green eyes. He had the same gaunt, hawklike face as my father, but he did not give me the impression of a man obsessed with arms and battle. I had felt his gaze during our stay at Cadbury, and I felt too that he might wish to enjoy me. But I comported myself with the dignity of a woman newly married to a lord.

During the journey from Cadbury to Gorlot, Uryens rode at the point of the company. He had appointed Accolon as my protector. Acconlon matched his horse's gait with mine and I silently admired his excellent horsemanship.

The weather changed noticeably as we moved northward, growing colder and heavily misted. There were great outcroppings of stone and strange odors from the bogs. The mists made evil shapes ahead of us. But when we rode into the vapors we could see that the evil shapes were simply gorse and trees. The landscape seemed more unfriendly than at Cadbury or Tintagel.

I found myself chilling in the wetness of the air, so I told Accolon to ask Uryens to halt. Accolon helped me to dismount and fetched my heavy leather cloak from one of my clothing packs. He helped me to fasten it and I remounted my horse. The white mists surrounded us all the while. I thanked him and received the most beautiful smile in reply.

The castle at Gorlot was unlike any other I had known. The stones of its walls were old and rough, and the wood crude and weatherbeaten. Uryens had prepared for my arrival, but not enough to accommodate my own more luxurious habits and needs. I set about to improve the comforts of the household by ordering the blacksmith to make new cooking utensils according to my designs, and I engaged the women of the household in fashioning leather and other materials for clothing, draperies, and bedding. Uryens was clearly pleased with my efforts. And you, Ceinwen, must remember that lovely winter's day when you, at last, could resume your own work on your tapestry frame.

✧

Our days at Gorlot were quite simple. Uryens was a rigorous taskmaster over his small force of warriors and drilled them daily. I watched him often and admired his direct manner, his skills, and his intelligence. I spent each morning in training myself as a physician by attending to the minor ailments of the women and children in the castle and village of Gorlot.

Our enjoyment at night was casual, without excitement. I did not wish to educate Uryens in what I knew about the possibilities of enjoyment. I did not love him, my marriage to him was not of my choosing. Four months after I arrived at Gorlot, Accolon became my secret lover, and then my beloved.

☼

During my marriage to Uryens I learned some secrets about the dreams of men and women. I learned that men, especially when they are engaged in a common effort, dream similar dreams.

These are the common dreams of men: The enjoyment of women. Victory in battle by the slaughter of other men. Luxury in everyday life. Playing at childrens' games to hide from their unwillingness to leave childhood, to honestly confront their destinies. What destinies? The destinies that our gods and goddesses bestow on each of us at birth: To live without raging at defeat. I had seen how not only bitter defeat, but also how a costly, bloody victory in battle can generate a fury that turns into rage against women.

Women, too, have common dreams, especially when they are of the same station in life. These are the common dreams of women: The enjoyment of men. The rearing of healthy, intelligent children. Quiet and peace in everyday life. To grow with love for each other. And, too often, the dream of revenge against cruel men, which must be kept hidden from them.

✿

In my workrooms at Tintagel, at Cadbury, and during those first months at Uryens' castle at Gorlot, I had found that doses of certain medicines made field mice, rabbits, and some dogs behave in ways unusual for their kind.

One medicine was a weak tea made from cotoneaster leaves. When I mixed the tea into the animals' drinking water they behaved with amazing affection for each other. They huddled together and licked each other as if they were loving parents caring for each other as children, ignorant of their true relationships.

I had used that tea in Orkney while I awaited the birthing of my son, Mordred. It had helped me to dream luxuriously.

✿

Arthur commanded Uryens to Cadbury, to prepare to ward off another Pict raid that had been reported by our spies. Uryens told me that Arthur had devised a plan that might for all time end the mad ravagings of our crops and women. Uryens had become an admirer of Arthur's leadership and stratagems. My beloved Accolon would of course accompany Uryens to Arthur's council.

Under the constraints of our unequal stations at Gorlot, Accolon and I had rid ourselves from the weight of dreams that color so many lovings. The dream of being together for eternity. The dream of a life together that would be filled with children and their happiness. We accepted the strictures of my marriage, which could be broken only by Uryens' or my own passage into the Other World. And both Accolon and I knew that if Uryens were to discover our secret enjoyments I would be punished by fire at the stake, and Accolon would be executed by beheading.

✩

I decided that I would try to stimulate and encourage the carnal lustings of Uryens and Arthur. Accolon agreed to help me. During our secret meetings, while Uryens slept the sleep of an exhausted farm horse, Accolon and I had enjoyed each other in ways I thought beyond the ken of even my gods and goddesses. I adored him, and he me. He would give his life to save mine, and I would give mine to save his.

☼

On the night before Uryens and his company were to depart for Cadbury, I gave Accolon a small packet of cotoneaster leaves and instructed him in the dosage and its effects.

I tried to follow their actions at Cadbury in my quicksilver mirror, but the images were not always clear. I thought that the strange weather at Gorlot might have affected the quicksilver. There were lightning and thunderstorms almost every day. Then, in the final days of their stay at Cadbury, the weather changed and my mirror became crystal clear for a few hours.

I saw that Arthur, Uryens, and Accolon were preparing to go on a hunt. I hoped urgently that Accolon would find some way to use the tea, but then the mirror clouded again. Nevertheless, during those last days at Cadbury, Accolon was able to make splendid use of the tea. He told me what happened when he returned to Gorlot.

Arthur had sighted a beautiful white stag that he was eager to add to his collection of rare animals. Arthur, Uryens, and Accolon went into the forest and tracked the stag's hoofprints for some hours. Then, tired and frustrated, they decided to rest at the bank of a pretty stream. While the others slept Accolon was able to pour some of the cotoneaster tea into Arthur's and Uryens's mead. When they awakened from their naps Arthur and Uryens drank some mead and resumed their search.

They found the white stag at the edge of the stream. But it was dying of an arrow wound inflicted by an unknown hunter. At the very moment that Arthur raised his lance to pierce the stag's heart, it lifted its head to look at Arthur and Uryens. Instantly, the two men fell to the earth in a deep, leaden sleep.

Accolon sat by fully awake, but kept his eyes half-closed so that he would not arouse their suspicion. In the mid-afternoon Arthur and Uryens awakened at the same moment, and each reported having had the same dream!

In their dream, as they were about to kill the dying stag a large, beautiful black boat rounded the curve in the stream.

When it came to the shore, twelve young women appeared and invited them into the boat.

Arthur and Uryens spoke excitedly of the maidens' garments of gossamer cloths in marvelous colors, of their naked bosoms high and firm with delicate nipples, and of the backs of their long skirts slit high to expose their smooth buttocks as they moved about.

They dreamed that the women entertained them with wonderful liquors and sweets, and then enjoyed the men in turn, on soft couches, while the boat floated gently all through the dreamed night.

Arthur and Uryens asked Accolon if he had dreamed as they had. When Accolon answered that his sleep was dreamless, they reminded each other that they were high noblemen after all, while Accolon was simply a warrior knight. Accolon behaved with modesty in the face of their jibes.

They brought the dead white stag back to Cadbury. Accolon and Uryens returned to Gorlot a few days later.

Late at night, encircled in each other's arms, Accolon and I giggled like children as he recounted the bewilderment and bragging pride of the two high noblemen.

☼

When he was not occupied with a mission to some other court, or had gone to Badon for a Druid council meeting, Merlin lived at Cadbury. He was the chief adviser to Arthur on governing, war making, and ceremonies. Arthur could not have had a better counselor, for Merlin held the wisdom of the ancients close in his mind. With his knowledge of past victories and defeats, Merlin could divine the outcome of his schemes if they were executed according to his devising.

Even though Arthur was now a Christian, he trusted Merlin and knew that his own position, as king of all the Britons, would be ensured by a Druid.

Arthur turned to the bishop for instruction in matters of the Christian faith. The bishop envied and disliked Merlin because of the influence he brought to Arthur's decisions. But the bishop also knew that his own influence would grow with time. So he behaved with courtesy to Merlin. I knew that the bishop spoke for Rome, just as Merlin spoke for me, for my goddesses and gods.

Arthur was certainly aware of the bishop's disapproval of Merlin's influence in the court. But Arthur had learned how to use the wisdom of both men. Arthur was a leader. The unification of the Britons was the shining aim that all three shared, each for his own interest.

✧

Both Merlin and the bishop were enchanter bards when they sat to entertain us with their tales of long ago. I remember listening to them when I was a child in Uther Pendragon's court, and later, before my banishment, at Arthur's.

Merlin would spin our minds with memories of violent skies and breathtaking visions of heroes, gods, and goddesses. The bishop told the stories of his one god, of Jesus Christ, of Mary, Christ's mother, who had conceived Jesus without enjoyment, and of the lives of Christ's friends, who were called his "disciples."

Arthur had never known his parents. After I had learned to enjoy Erec and Merlin, I sometimes thought that Arthur may have found comfort in the unspoken meanings of the bishop's story of the birth of Jesus. Perhaps those stories had moved Arthur to the Christian faith. Perhaps there were too many Druid gods and goddesses for Arthur, a king, to embrace.

But I knew, I remembered how Arthur had been conceived so cruelly by Uther on my own mother. I would fix my mind and eyes on Arthur's face as he listened to the bishop's stories. When he had drunk more than enough mead, he became quiet and thoughtful. He sometimes reached to hold Guinevere's hand while the bishop recounted the cruelties inflicted upon Christians long ago. The murders and crucifixions of believers by nonbelievers. The torturing of simple people who had begun to imagine deliverance from enslavement, and their belief in the promise of a peaceful place they called heaven. I would forget my anger against Arthur in those moments.

But I could not forget what I saw when I was a little girl on that night in my parents' bedchamber at Tintagel.

☼

Merlin's stories cast spells on all of us. Even the rowdiest, noisiest knights would stare blindly, as did Arthur, while their minds were ensnared in Merlin's great visions. His training as a Druid enabled him to remember and tell the history of humankind from its beginning on this earth. Most wonderful were his stories of the gods and goddesses that nourished every living thing, every stone and stream and mountain and meadow, every child, woman, and man.

Merlin's stories reached into our guts and heated our blood to make us quiver with excitement. Merlin would make us see that whatever work we did, every day, could blossom into something wonderful.

☼

Erec had found a simple way to keep me informed about events at Cadbury. Messengers were sent to Uryens and the other liege lords each week, to keep them alert to Arthur's problems and decisions. Erec would instruct the messengers to bring his private reports to me. They were always brief, but very useful.

Erec's messages told of disturbing happenings at Cadbury. I learned that a young, brilliant warrior named Lancelot, from Brittany, had been taken into the company of the Knights of the Round Table, that he was absolutely invincible in every trial with sword or lance, and that his archery was beyond compare. And that Lancelot had become Guinevere's favorite knight.

Gawain, Morgause's oldest son, had been made a knight of the Round Table about a year before Lancelot. Gawain had quickly proved himself superb in matters of arms, and Arthur placed him at his right at the Round Table. Now Lancelot's superior mastery of arms had begun to gnaw at Gawain's pride.

Just as I had imagined, the bond that Arthur had hoped to form with his Knights of the Round Table could be wrenched, perhaps broken, by the arousal of envy. No matter how pure they were considered to be, the Round Table knights were men, after all.

Thinking about the other strange things that Erec reported, I slowly began to understand that they could have been devised only by Merlin. Merlin would use his white magic to warn Arthur against relaxing the ideals he had championed as a young king.

Merlin would have understood that Guinevere's fondness for Lancelot could ignite a fire that would be dangerous for Arthur and his court. Merlin would not warn Arthur directly about so personal a matter. But he could insinuate his visions of danger to Arthur by arranging those strange happenings.

✿

Ceinwen, I am almost certain that it was Merlin who dazzled Arthur's court with those pantomimes. Did they actually happen? Couldn't Merlin, with his great skill, have drugged the assemblies and told them stories? How could he have made them so real? I don't know.

But I can easily imagine Merlin's use of potions to bring the supper assembly into trance, while he described the silent intrusions of strange visitors and their strange behavior. I remember too well the enchantment of Merlin's voice. And I smiled when I imagined the bishop's shock and consternation at the pagan displays that would appear in Cadbury's great hall, out of nowhere.

✿

I also remember how I had grown ever more bitter at my own helplessness in my wish to punish Arthur for his smiling, harsh dismissal from his court and councils, for banishing me to Gorlot.

✪

Merlin was an absolute master of disguise, a skill absolutely necessary for his protection. He would travel from Cadbury on missions for Arthur. If he were recognized as Merlin, he risked attack by those disaffected Britons who continued to resist Arthur's grand schemes.

Merlin's favorite disguise transformed him into an old, feeble beggar who wandered from castle to castle. And as a Druid priest, Merlin would conduct certain rituals wearing the skin and head of a white stag.

Of course I was never a witness to those fantastic morality tales at Arthur's court. But one of Erec's reports became fixed in my memory. I believe it is now time for me to tell it.

✪

Early one evening while the lords, knights and their ladies were drinking and carousing in the great hall, a white stag and a lean, black hound suddenly rushed in, astonishing the assembly. The animals were closely followed by two strangers, a young, golden-haired lady and a black-haired, tall knight. Gawain, besotted, flew into a rage at the strangers' discourteous intrusion. Claiming the defense of Arthur's honor he drew his sword and engaged the stranger knight in a vicious fight.

Neither the knight nor Gawain were properly armored, so the duel swiftly became a bloody one. Arthur, Guinevere, and the assembly sat in silence as they were spattered with flying drops of blood.

Suddenly the lady moved to protect the stranger knight by stepping between him and Gawain. Furiously thrusting his sword and shouting at her to get out of his way, Gawain hacked at her neck and decapitated the lady. Her head rolled on the floor to Gawain's feet. Neither the stranger knight nor the lady had said a word during the encounter.

Aroused by the smell of blood, the hound leaped to bite at the stag's hindquarter and then trotted calmly out of the great hall with a piece of the stag's flesh hanging from its jaw. The bloodied stranger knight lifted the headless lady's body, gently guided the limping stag out of the great hall, and went out into the darkness. Arthur roared for the servants to come into the hall and clean it.

The frightened servants, puzzled at finding no trace of blood anywhere, nevertheless obeyed Arthur's strange command and silently swabbed the tables and floor.

I can only believe that Merlin had mixed one of his potions into the mead that was to be served in the hall that evening. So all the men and women were affected. In their poisoned dream, the knights denounced Gawain, for he had killed an innocent woman.

The knights insisted that Gawain be punished by carrying the woman's severed head in a sling around his neck.

But when the assembly finally recovered, no severed head could be found in the great hall.

☼

I have thought long and deeply about that horrible vision. I can only conclude that Merlin had divined the future corruption and collapse of Arthur's reign, and that he wished to alert Arthur to that possibility.

Gawain, so handsome and so fine a warrior, eager to challenge the strange knight's unbidden entry! Was it not the custom at Cadbury to open its doors to strangers? What made Gawain so violent in that unnecessary duel? Was he displaying his zeal to be superior to Lancelot by being the first to rise in defense of Arthur?

Why did the lords and knights remain silent and motionless, watching that murderous sword fight until its horrible end, not one of them rising to halt the bloodshed?

The beautiful white stag, an animal so rare and so desirable for Arthur's collection! Only after the two men had drawn each other's blood did the hound leap to tear meat from the stag's flank. Had Merlin insinuated that men, warriors, can become beasts in the wild fury of battle? But animals usually kill others only when they are hungry. And men? Men kill for pride, for power, for ownership.

The strange lady, who so pitifully tried to protect her knight? Who was she? Was she every woman who wishes to protect the life of her beloved in battle, so often in vain? Was that the reason for the loss of her head, the place of her thinking and knowing?

And the strange knight? Could he have been the image of Lancelot in Merlin's scheme to teach Arthur's court about true valor, true fidelity, true courtesy?

And lastly, Arthur. How could he sit silently observing poor Gawain so eagerly, wildly offering his life to save Arthur's? Did Arthur relish that terrible sword fight and the splilling of blood?

Had Merlin placed the entire assembly under an enchantment?

Was Merlin beginning to retreat from Arthur's councils?

✿

I recall the rumors that I, Morgain, had been seen--actually seen!--in the course of other fantastic adventures that humiliated Arthur, dear Gawain, and others of the court.

Ever since my banishment from Cadbury, I have lived either at Tintagel or at Gorlot, unable to travel alone. Merlin, with his gifts for disguise, could have become me, or he could have chosen a Druid priestess to become me. Merlin's wild enchantments and devices would give pause to Arthur in his high ambition, or at least alert him to his own weaknesses.

✿

Mordred. My son.

Morgause reported to me as often as she could about my son's growth and behavior. Mordred thought of Gawain, Gaheris, and Ewain as his older brothers, and Morgause and Loth had been careful to nourish that idea. Gawain was now Arthur's most trusted knight. And Gaheris and Ewain were also at Cadbury, in training as warriors in Arthur's army.

Morgause told me of Mordred's unusual intelligence and his burning ambition to become a knight like his brothers in Arthur's Round Table. But she also told of Mordred's faults: his sudden angers, and his impatience with obstacles of any kind. She remarked on the boy's physical strength, that it was greater than her sons', even though Mordred was not as heavily muscled as they were.

Loth was more lenient with Mordred than he had been with his own sons. But there were occasions when he found it impossible to rein Mordred without a thrashing. Afterward, Mordred would become manageable and would realize how sorely he had tried Loth's patience. So Mordred and Loth developed a cautious affection for each other.

In one message to Morgause I asked whether the red stain on the boy's face had faded. Morgause replied that it had not, that it was a deep discoloration, a permanent birthmark. I did not pursue that question. But I carried an ache in my spirit that brought me to tears when I thought of the boy's disgust and anger whenever he was reminded of the mark he would wear all the days of his life. How could he disregard it? How did other men see him? And how would it affect his wish to enjoy a woman when the time came for him?

I sent a message to Morgause to find a young woman to enjoy Mordred, and she did. Morgause treated the young woman, a daughter of one of the farmers, kindly, and Mordred was happier and calmer for some time. I never learned the young woman's name. Morgause wished to protect her.

When Mordred reached his sixteenth winter Loth sent him to Cadbury to train in the skills of war. Erec kept me informed of Mordred's progress. I was happy to learn of Mordred's eager mastery of arms, his quick wit, and his controlled, intense passion in the execution of every task.

☼

Erec's curiosity about my interest in Mordred was satisfied when I told him that Mordred was my youngest nephew, the son of Morgause and Loth. Erec then told me something that gave me great pleasure. Erec said that young Sir Mordred, who had just been knighted, was ever eager to hear the stories of Arthur's battles and the wars that had been fought by Uther Pendragon. When he was not engaged in the practice of sword and lance Mordred sought out the older knights and lords, like Ulfius, to hear them tell their experiences in battle. Erec had overheard Mordred's questions and was astonished at the range of his wisdom.

☼

Arthur, Uryens, and many other lords had now firmly joined their forces to fight our enemies, the Picts, the Irish, and the Saxons. Arthur was accepted as the true leader of the Britons. He had proven his skills in the training of our armies, in his negotiations with the Angle and Celtic lords, and by his wise and just accommodation of their often conflicting needs and demands.

But as we Britons grew in numbers and loyalty to each other, so too did our enemies. Their raids became more massive and sometimes devastating, just as our repulsions grew more violent and punitive. But our warriors had the great advantage of being trained to fight on horse as well as on foot. The Picts, the Irish, and the Saxon raiders had to fight on foot. So our horse-mounted lancers, swordsmen, and archers made swift havoc of the enemy forces, again and again.

I was able to watch some of those bloody encounters in my quicksilver mirror, but only when they took place in bright daylight. Our enemies usually raided our stores of grain, flax, wool, and honey under the cover of night. But despite their savagery, they could not take possession of our lands. Only a few captives were allowed to remain in Britain, usually Saxons unable to get aboard their retreating ships. They were kept to work as farm slaves or as sheepherders. Enemy warriors who were wounded and unable to escape were killed or left to die on the fields of battle.

Far more painful to me was the Saxon's abduction of our women and children from our farmlands. They were never seen again. From Accolon, a Scot himself, I learned to hate them and their allies.

Uryens, my husband, and Accolon, my lover, would leave Gorlot with their small army to fight the raiders in our sector. After the battles our warrior leaders met at Arthur's Cadbury to account for the losses of men, women, children, and food stores.

When Uryens returned to Gorlot after such meetings he would recount the splendid defenses by our warriors, and then the numbers of our losses. I listened to those accounts and grew to pity my husband. His life had become carnage and survival, losses and victories.

✿

You, Ceinwen, and Taw, my raven, were the closest beings to me in those lonely days at Gorlot. Niniane, the young singer whom I brought to Gorlot from Arthur's court, might have become another friend. But she had cleverly kept me at a distance. She learned to help me in my workroom, and we made many new healing potions of herbs, roots, and powdered rocks. She was always eager to have me talk of what I knew of Druid magical potions. But I did not encourage those questions.

I had grown accustomed to her refusal of confidences, and I simply accepted her diligence as reason enough to keep her in our court.

Taw, my raven, was usually at ease in our workroom. But sometimes I saw his frantic scurrying to escape the stinks that steamed up from our potions. I would gesture to him to go to the window slit. He would poke his head out into the open air until we had finished our work. He soon learned to go there of his own accord.

Unable to fly, he had learned to entertain me with a spiralling dance that he performed while I sang "Taw, Taw, caw, caw, caw. Taw, Taw, law, law, law." His amber eyes flashed and closed. He would wobble from side to side, and I would become softly enchanted with the wonder of his secret, animal life. I cherished his presence in my workroom and often told him my own secrets.

I did not realize how much I loved him until the day he disappeared from my workroom. I noticed that the door, usually closed, had been left open. Taw was not in the room. I ran through the corridor calling his name. Outdoors the grounds were covered by a thin layer of snow and ice. I ran along the road away from the castle gate. Just ahead I could see a small, black heap on the white snow. Taw lay there, lifeless, with a trickle of blood oozing from the back of his head. Close by, I found a stone like those that boys use in their slingshots. Taw's blood had frozen on the little stone.

I carried Taw back to the castle and gave him to a grounds keeper to bury him near the castle wall. My tears began to flow after I had locked myself in my workroom, alone in my luxurious prison.

Early next morning I dressed in my warmest cloak and sheepskin surcoat to go out to Taw's grave. The air was terribly cold and mists floated in wild shapes. The sun had not yet risen. I walked with my hand touching the castle wall, touching my way in the fog to find Taw's grave. It was no larger than a small child's, the little mound of dark earth oddly like a gaping hole in the surrounding white snow.

I could not hold back my sobs and tears. My legs weakened and I slowly sank to sit on the snow. Taw! My strange friend, Taw.

As always, my weeping slowly exhausted my sadness, and for a little while I could think of nothing. I saw only that dark mound in the white snow.

Then, with a rush, new thoughts arose to command my attention. Why had I become so fond of an injured raven? How could I have talked to Taw as if he truly understood me? Did he really understand my words? Or had he heard the rise and fall of my speech and my mutterings, like the music I could sometimes hear among people?

I had always thought that Taw understood what I said to him. But now I realized that, within me, I had a raven, a black, angry bird.

From some place in the back of my skull I heard my voice singing, "Taw, Taw, caw, caw, caw," and I saw his awkward dance.

He had not danced to please me. He had danced because he had accompanied the raven in me when I sang the music that was ours.

☼

I could not rid myself of the image of the raven within me. For several days and nights I paced my workroom floor with a flaming red rage coloring my every thought and feeling. I saw Taw, my dependent and my confidence keeper, grow taller and take the proportions of a large man, black and fierce, ugly and gentle, loving me without reserve or question.

I loved Accolon, but our enjoyment had to be secret. My husband, Uryens, was obsessed with the protection of our lands, and with his undisguised pleasure in the daily anticipation of battle.

As my love of Accolon deepened, so too was I growing disgusted with Uryens and his animal coupling. I remember one night when, after Uryens had satisfied his bullish lust, I turned and whispered "Taw, Taw, caw, caw, caw." Uryens, spent with his enjoyment, had collapsed on our bed. He mumbled, "What, what?" I did not answer and he sank into his customary, sodden sleep.

☼

Ceinwen, please hear me out, I know that what I am saying may disgust you. But I am telling you about the madness in me that I remember. I cannot account for my whispering those sounds. They came to my mouth from somewhere deep inside me.

☼

Something in me had broken. I knew that I was losing control of my thoughts and my feelings. The world had closed around me, Gorlot with its mists and bogs, the dismal fortress it had always been, the unending sameness of my life outside my workroom, all had glutted me so that I no longer could speak. I often retched.

On the morning after that terrible night, I decided to send Niniane back to Cadbury. I did not want her help any longer.

She was too closed into herself to become my friend. I told her that I would ask Sir Cai to find a place for her in the household and to treat her kindly. She left Gorlot that afternoon. I sent a young warrior with her for her protection during the journey.

☼

I did not sleep that night. I was pacing back and forth, imitating Taw's walk and dance, when I heard a loud, ripping noise in my head.

I felt Accolon's dear arms around me as he helped me back to my bedchamber. He whispered that he had been awakened by my movement in the corridor, that I was holding a long knife high above my head, that I was about to enter Uryens' bedchamber, that my eyes were mad and unseeing, that he grasped my wrist and took the knife out of my hand, and that he would put me to bed and sit with me until daybreak.

I did not remember having done anything of what he told me. And, if I indeed intended to kill Uryens, I felt neither remorse, nor relief that I had not done so. In my mind, I had already killed Uryens, my jailer.

I remained bedridden for a number of days, exhausted and weak. You were so kind, Ceinwen, as ever.

In the evening, after sleeping through most of the daylight hours, I would awaken to see Uryens sitting in a corner of my room, silently gazing at me. He seemed to be in a somber, morbid state, but I did not speak to him. I pretended that I was asleep.

On those evenings Accolon waited until he heard Uryens go back to his own bedchamber. Then he would come to my room and hold me closely while I cried, bewildered by the frightening shifts between clarity and the horrifying images in my mind.

I saw meadows and forests glistening with freshly spilled blood. I saw the dismembered bodies of warriors and women and children still alive, all moving toward each other to form mounds of bone and flesh. I watched buzzards hovering in the air above and small animals crowding to approach the hacked chests and heads and arms and legs. In my moments of clarity I knew that I had seen all of our lives and deaths, and our helplessness in changing them.

✩

In the spring of that year I recovered enough strength to ride my horse again, but only at a walking pace. I thought about what I might do to achieve sanity, and my mind grew clearer as I realized that I wished for it. The meadows and forests began to bloom with grasses and leaves, and I soaked myself in their greenness. The soft, early morning mists lifted like curtains to reveal fields of newly planted grains, and I saw patches of brilliant red poppies.

My aim had been to annoy and humiliate Arthur, Guinevere, and the fellowship of the Round Table. Those intentions now seemed like the games of a spiteful child. I decided then to try to teach Arthur and his company of warriors the true meaning of death. I would offer death to them as an individual choice, without the cloak of valor or courage or the claim of the necessity of defending our lands against our enemies.

☼

Uryens had become Arthur's most loyal and devoted ally. He was away from Gorlot more and more frequently, steadily gaining Arthur's confidence and comradeship in planning the defenses against the Picts and Saxons. Arthur's strategies for resisting the hated invaders had made their raids less frequent, because they were repelled so viciously and lost so many of their warriors.

Armed, devastating combat had become the chief aim of the lords and knights at Arthur's court. They prepared themselves by elaborate exercises with sword and lance, on foot and on horse, by hunting with bows and arrows, by feasting grossly, and by drinking great quantities of mead.

You, Ceinwen, were my only companion in those days. You will remember my raging, wild anger at my imprisonment at Gorlot.

☆

One day Uryens returned from Cadbury, robust and happy after hunting in the forests near the castle. In the evening we sat before a clean fire in the hearth. I listened to his tales of tracking and killing deer and wild boars, enough meat, he proudly said, to feed the men of the Round Table for several weeks. His face glowed with the remembrance of the chase and the kills.

I said something simple in praise of his deeds. Then I asked him bluntly to allow me to leave Gorlot, to live at Tintagel. He was silent for some time.

Staring into the flames, Uryens asked me why I wished to leave him. I replied that my life at Gorlot had become bitter, that I did not feel myself to be his wife, that I wished to live in a place where I could breathe. I said that I had become an object to satisfy his lust, and that I did not wish to offend him by my indifference, as I knew I eventually would. I told him that I knew him to be kind and gentle, but I was unable to love him. Silent and somber, he turned to look at me.

After a long silence he asked me when I wished to leave. I replied that I would go as soon as he gave me permission. He said that he had been aware of my dissatisfaction for some time, that he felt unable to change himself to make me love him; he would indeed permit me to leave Gorlot because he loved and cherished me, and wished me to live in grace and peace.

I looked at him gratefully. My eyes brimmed with tears and I blurted out my wish to take Accolon with me to Tintagel.

He replied that he would permit that, too, and that he had been aware of our secret meetings for some time. He did not look at me. I moved to him and kissed his cheek. I thanked him for his goodness and walked out of the room. The heavy stones in my chest dissolved in the sudden flood of air, pure and sweet, that filled my being.

✿

Accolon and I settled into our new life at Tintagel with great joy. We were careful to keep our situation as unmarried lovers as discreet as possible. We agreed to avoid making any sign of our affection visible to members of my court, or to the small company of warriors, artisans, and servants. We found ourselves delighted and challenged by our resolve to conduct ourselves as equals. And those constraints in our public lives seemed to intensify our private passion for each other.

☼

I called for an assembly of all who worked or resided at the court and asked them to help make Tintagel a place of quiet and peace. I declared Accolon to be Tintagel's defender, responsible for organizing and training our small group of warriors.

I remember your pleasure, Ceinwen, when I told the assembly that you were to resume your duties as mistress of household affairs at Tintagel.

Accolon and I agreed that, as the defender of Tintagel, his chamber should be close to mine. I asked him to use my parents' room as his own, and I reoccupied my own bedchamber, next to his. I never revealed to him what I had witnessed as a child, years ago, standing at the connecting door. He would come to my bed at night.

I cleared my workroom of the old leaves, animal bones, and other reminders of my childhood pastimes. I was now determined to develop my powers in magic for sorcery.

✿

Arthur and Cadbury Castle were now closer. When Accolon rode to Cadbury to receive instructions on the defense of Tintagel I asked him to invite Erec to Tintagel. I was eager to offer Arthur the means for his own death, and I would need Erec for my plan.

✿

The Great Water Carrier, the sign of my birth, has passed in the sky forty-seven times, counting the forty-seven years of my life. If I had been born to the family of a farmer, I would have passed over into the Otherworld long before now, when I tell all this.

I have lived my life in castles, near closed villages where so many good, intelligent young peasant maidens enter into stupid, insufferable marriages, birth too many children, grow stiff and wrinkled with endless labor and care, and then die in their early womanhood. I have seen their faces, rigid with the bitter acceptance of their lot as they were lowered into their graves.

I was protected from such a life by my birth into a noble family. I look calmly to my passage into the Other World after I have finished the telling of my terrible deeds. I knew nothing of backbreaking labor, nor have I suffered the pain of loving without being loved by the man I loved. But the suffering I experienced in my mind, my madness during the years I am about to recount, was enough to make me weep now with pity for all women whose souls and minds live in pain.

☼

I must resume my telling.

I know now that in those years at Tintagel there were two Morgains. One was the Morgain deeply happy to love and be loved by Accolon, if for only a brief time. The other Morgain was an angry, raucous raven, a poisonous spirit, malevolent. I was consumed with my intention to practice black magic. I simply could not rid myself of my blazing, blinding rage at Arthur and Guinevere for dismissing my claim to high status in the court at Cadbury Castle.

With no warning sign, every day--every day!--during those early years at Tintagel I would hear a painful, tearing sound followed by a strange sensation behind my eyes, as if my brain had been cut by a heavy, dull knife.

Then I would walk slowly, half blind, to my workroom and sit at my table. I tried to rid myself of the bewilderment and dull pain by drinking potions. A potion made from the violet flowers of the spiderwort became my favorite.

The pain would lessen and a flood of images would intrigue me with their variety and strangeness. I searched for ways to make such images become real.

One day, utterly wild with the promise of one such image, I took one of your tapestries, dear Ceinwen, and fashioned it into a surcoat to fit Arthur's tall frame. I remembered that years before I had learned that quicksilver, when heated, gave off terrible, deadly fumes. I had seen two lovely sparrows fall lifeless when they were tied by their claws to a stand next to my heating dish.

I fastened a small sack filled with quicksilver into each of the seams that joined the surcoat's sleeves to the shoulders.

I imagined Arthur wearing the surcoat, the heat from his armpits warming the quicksilver, and his sudden death.

A few weeks later Erec came to Tintagel, carrying instructions from Arthur to Accolon. While Accolon went off to talk with Huw, our armorer, I asked Erec to take the surcoat to Arthur as a sign of my wish to win his friendship again. Erec proudly replied that because of his position as Arthur's squire it would be unseemly for him to do so. He suggested that someone from Tintagel should bear the gift to Arthur.

I then asked Erec if he would escort Rhiain, a young woman from our village, to present the surcoat to Arthur. I knew Rhiain to be at ease on horse, and that her face, her simple speech, and her fine bearing would impress Arthur and his lords. Erec agreed to escort her to Cadbury.

My quicksilver mirror showed me what happened at Cadbury Castle when Rhiain offered the surcoat to Arthur. She did so with shy grace. Arthur smiled and expressed his pleasure at my wish to make amends for my offense to the court. Rhiain told him that I had asked that he test the surcoat's fitting. Arthur arose to take it from her hands. But Merlin, sitting next to Arthur, quietly told him to ask Rhiain to be the first to try it, so that Arthur could see its decorations.

Two servants helped Rhiain into the surcoat, which was heavy and rather stiff. Arthur asked Rhiain to walk to and fro so that he could see the way the surcoat fell from the shoulders. Rhiain did so with the lovely grace of a tall, well-made young woman.

I watched with horror as Rhiain stopped pacing.

She sank to the floor shuddering violently. In the turmoil that followed I watched Merlin, who had remained in his seat. He smiled faintly as he observed the servants remove Rhiain's body from the hall. I saw his eyes widen for a moment and then close in reflection.

I turned away from my quicksilver mirror, retching and sobbing.

Then you, Ceinwen, rushed into my work-room. You held me close and asked what had cast me into such a state. When I had calmed and was able to speak, I told you that I had killed Rhiain. I told you everything, how I had used your tapestry to make the surcoat, how I had poisoned it with the intention to kill Arthur, and how poor Rhiain had become the victim of my madness. And that I was now certain that Merlin had divined my murderous intention.

☼

You nod "yes" now, and I see the tears brimming in your eyes.

Ceinwen, write this too. What happened to me happened to you as well. Write this down!

In the evening of the day of Rhiain's death, you came to my bedchamber and told me that you had decided to take the vow of silence, never to speak again lest you might reveal what you had learned of my madness.

How I wish that you would release me, that you would speak to me again. You shake your head, "No."

But I know that your devotion to me all these years has been a twisted forgiving, even as you write this.

☼

For months after I killed poor Rhiain my mind was empty, empty of passion and thought. There were some days when I felt that my mind was healing, in retreat from that other, black-shadowed Morgain. I rode out every morning, in every weather, making myself an animal at one with Delyth, my beautiful mare.

I breathed Tintagel's air hungrily. My nose tingled with the delicious smells of the ocean mists, the sweet grasses of its meadows and hills, and even the sharp gases rising from the bogs.

After my midday meal I would sleep through the afternoon. I had no wish to use my quicksilver mirror, or to make new potions. At night, in my bed, Accolon and I often slept without enjoying each other. Then I would urge him out of his gentleness into the ferocity of a wild, greedy stallion. We became each other's captives.

Accolon was now in his virile, commanding maturity. I would watch from the parapet as he drilled our small group of warriors in the skills he had learned from Uryens and Arthur at Cadbury. Accolon would become his sword, he would become his lance, he became the arrow flying to its target. Our warriors admired him and learned swiftly to win his encouragement and praise. It was Accolon's mastery and his kindness that brought many young sons of farmers into the company of Tintagel warriors.

He was now truly a wonderful man, attending smoothly to his tasks as the defender of Tintagel and happy in the days and nights of his life. We had agreed not to have a child, although I felt certain that he secretly wished for one. But I had no desire to change my life for that purpose.

☼

Early one morning we awakened smiling at each other. We had slept with my arm around his neck, and I breathed his skin, his sweat, and his rare, spiced breath. I whispered close to his ear that I loved him endlessly. He murmured with pleasure.

With the utmost ease, the next words coming from my lips were those of the other Morgain. I heard her ask him if he thought himself capable of winning a duel against Arthur, now that he had learned so much from him.

Accolon awakened fully, as surprised as I was by my question. After a few moments he nodded, yes. But he did not see how or why he should challenge Arthur. I reassured him by telling him a lie, that my question had arisen from an idle image that I had seen in my dreaming.

Throughout that morning, riding alone through patches of fog broken by shafts of clean sunlight, I toyed with my questions.

I kept Delyth reined to a walk. The mists rolling in from the ocean and the mare's deliberate gait seemed to help me search for the question's meaning.

What did that other Morgain wish? The death of Arthur? Accolon's death? Or Arthur's humiliation by my lover? Would Guinevere grieve for Arthur, now that she had taken Lancelot as her secret lover? What might happen to me if Accolon were to kill Arthur? Could Accolon indeed be the victor in such a duel?

And what if Arthur were to kill Accolon?

The questions roiled in my head as I sat at the midday meal. I began to feel ill and my eyes started to play uncomfortable tricks. I excused myself and went to my bedchamber hoping to sleep.

"Could Accolon be the victor in such a duel?" repeated itself over and over. I was unable to fall asleep. Without warning, I heard that ripping noise in my brain. I left my bedchamber and walked dizzily to my workroom. I had kept an essence of the spiderwort potion in a bottle, and I carefully prepared a dose.

My hands shook as I drank it. The pain behind my eyes lessened at last, and then a flow of images flooded my brain.

I saw how Accolon could kill Arthur. I would have to replace Arthur's invincible sword, Excalibur, with an imitation of it. Our armorer, Huw, was very skillful and could make such an imitation. Then I had to find some way for Accolon to use the real Excalibur. It could happen in one of the warrior training tournaments. As was the custom, the squires would give the swords to Arthur and Accolon after they had helmeted themselves. So I had to enlist Erec's help. I knew that his lust for me had slept in his body, dreaming to enjoy me again. He would agree to help me if I were to offer him the enjoyment we had known secretly, years ago. He would be visiting Tintagel in a few weeks to bring messages from Arthur.

Now all that was left was to realize my plan. I fell into a dreamless sleep.

✡

Erec was easily persuaded by my offer of enjoyment. We rode together one morning over the greening meadows. Without warning I veered into the forest. In the sunlit clearing I dismounted and quickly shed my clothes. The morning air was deliciously cool. When Erec rode into the clearing I opened my arms and asked him to warm me, just as I had when we were young.

He overcame his surprise and embraced me. As soon as he entered me he began to cry and moan his adoration. He spent himself quickly and collapsed.

When his trembling subsided I told him of my plan for the duel. I said that if he refused to help me I would accuse him of having raped me, and Accolon would certainly kill him.

He began to sob again, begging me to not to involve him, but I was resolute. He held me tightly, sobbing. When he stopped crying he said that he would help in my plan. He asked that I allow him to enter me again. I abandoned myself to enjoying him as I had when we were young.

✡

A congress of Arthur's liege lords and their knights provided the opportunity to try my plan. I had persuaded Accolon to be prepared to use Excalibur, and Erec had promised that Arthur would be given the fine imitation that Huw had forged. Accolon of course knew that Excalibur had made Arthur invincible. But he was wary of the outcome because he knew how skillful a swordsman Arthur could be. He had seen Arthur often enough in the vicious routs of our enemies.

But Accolon also knew that if he could subdue Arthur in the bout, he and I could marry without fear of Arthur's, or Merlin's, or the bishop's authority.

I watched the duel in my quicksilver mirror. Accolon was the first to accept Arthur's challenge for an exercise with swords. Arthur's first sword stroke slashed Accolon's right thigh and he fell to the ground, bleeding terribly from the wound, but he held Excalibur to parry Arthur's following thrust. Arthur's sword shattered when it struck Excalibur. Accolon collapsed, helpless, with Excalibur still in his grasp. Arthur paused for a moment, absorbing the deception.

He wrenched Excalibur out of Accolon's grip, stared at it, exploded into a roaring curse, and killed Accolon with a furious cut at his unprotected neck. As Arthur turned to face the spectators I saw Erec mount his horse and gallop madly away from Cadbury.

Accolon's body was carried back to Tintagel in a filthy wagon the following day, escorted by ten Round Table knights with Arthur's pennants flying from their lances. The wagon was left inside the castle gate and the knights silently dismounted.

They dragged Huw out of the armory and tied him to a post. Still maintaining their terrifying silence, each knight approached with his drawn sword and made one cut at Huw's head. Our warriors, our artisans, their wives and children, a few farmers standing at their wagons loaded with sheep and vegetables for the castle, all stood mute as they watched Huw die.

I remember the sound of sheep bleating in the silence. I gasped for air, boiling and suffocating with the horror of what I had done.

☼

It was Diarmid, Accolon's second in command, who saw me collapse and fall to the ground, and who carried me to my bedchamber. You knew, dear Ceinwen, how much, how desperately I wished to pass into the Other World. You kept me locked in my bedchamber and sealed my workroom to prevent my taking a potion to begin that passage.

When I began to recover I remember that you brought Elwyn, our bard, to my bedchamber to sing and play on his harp. One of his songs burned its way into my memory. I say it now. My eyes are dry, but I say it now,

> *short were their lives, and long the*
> *mourning left to their kinsmen . . .*
> *in battle they made women widows,*

*and many a mother with tears at
her eyelids.*

I stayed in my bed for weeks, mourning, empty. When I was able to walk about I asked you to tell our Druid to visit me.

I explained my wretched state to him, and my responsibility for it. I asked him to hear and accept my vow to remain forever chaste. He anointed my brow with the juice of mistletoe berries, and I declared that I would never again seek enjoyment with a man.

Each night before I go to sleep I call on my goddesses to care for Accolon in the Other World. I spend each day devoted to the welfare of the inhabitants of Tintagel, and to the care of men and women, knights and ladies, beggars and priests, and children who have somehow lost their way in their movement through this life. Tintagel, once my parents' beloved castle, is now an inn and a hospital.

☼

Merlin's wisdom and ability to see the future were the obstacles to my old, bitter, black aim to seek revenge against Arthur. Merlin had suspected my rankling ambition ever since that day in the forest grove, when he told me that he had been charged by the council of Druids with the responsibility of preparing Arthur to assume the British throne.

I had been unable to do any more than annoy Arthur with my spiteful plans. Accolon's death had lifted me, at last, out of the agony of revenge. I knew, somehow, that Merlin would always be able to parry my thrusts.

The terrible splitting noises and wild images in my head have ceased. And I have become a good physician.

☼

Surprisingly, Merlin's influence in Arthur's court grew with the enlargement of Arthur's domain. I believe that Merlin's eminence in the fellowship of Druids provided him with a web of spies, Druids who continue to practice despite our people's gradual acceptance of the Christian beliefs. And I continue to hold to my gods and goddesses, as Merlin taught me when I was a child. I have not found reason to change.

I cannot prove this, but I think that my inn was visited several times by Merlin in disguise. Merlin would want to be alert to whatever I might be doing or planning, and such visits could be useful to him and to Arthur. Merlin could change his face and shift his shape at will. I would never be able to outwit him.

☼

I have not seen Mordred since he was a four-year old boy playing in Morgause's garden when I visited her in the Orkneys almost twenty summers ago. Morgause had introduced me to Mordred as her sister, his aunt. I was quick to recover from the shock of his birthmark, and my affection for him grew deeper each day I was there. It was terribly disturbing to watch my intense little boy, so innocent of our lives' bonds, playing at war games with Morgause's sons.

When he reached the age of seventeen Mordred was accepted into the Round Table. Morgause proudly told me how Arthur had been impressed by my son's intelligence and rhetoric, as well as his skill at arms. At the end of his first year at Cadbury, Arthur sent him as his courier on important missions to lords in Brittany and Normandy. Mordred was rewarded with a lordship and was given some land near the eastern coast.

✿

Erec had disappeared from Cadbury after Accolon's death. But some of the other squires continued to inform me of the developing sickness in Arthur's court.

Launcelot, the French knight, had placed himself and Guinevere in mortal danger. This news excited me, but I was angered by the squires' crude pleasure as they rumored their imagined, lecherous details of Lancelot and Guinevere's secret enjoyments.

I accepted their reports in silence and thanked them.

Merlin would have known of Guinevere's and Lancelot's desperate, secret enjoyments. I understood Merlin's reluctance to alert Arthur, whom he loved as a son, and the wrenching pity he must have felt for all three of them. For Lancelot had proven to be intensely loyal to Arthur in all other respects.

But four of the Round Table lords, including Uryens and Mordred, envied Lancelot. I think they may have lusted for Guinevere themselves. While Arthur and some of his lords had left Cadbury to meet with Lodegrance at Camarthen, the four lords decided to expose the lovers.

They went to Guinevere's bedchamber one night, broke open the door, and surprised Lancelot in her room. Both were naked.

Lancelot rushed to clothe himself and then drew his sword.

He fought the intruders and killed young Aliers in his furious escape. He rode off into the forest and must have roamed for days without food. His wanderings brought him to a beach

near Tintagel, where two farmers found him
unconscious and brought him to my hospital.

☼

I had never seen Lancelot before. One of
my squires had identified him after he had been
washed and put to bed. When I learned who he
was I had him moved into a secret cell, to prevent
his discovery by Merlin or by Arthur's knights.

Lancelot had escaped with a deep sword
cut on his forehead. He remained unconscious
for about a week. I heard the stirring whisper of
loving within me while I treated his wound each
day.

He was a beautiful man indeed. His angu-
lar, bony face reminded me of my own Accolon.
But I had learned that I must carefully see the
difference between love and pity.

I ordered two young squires to guard his
room day and night. I swore them to secrecy on
pain of imprisonment.

I do not think that Lancelot was simply
asleep during those weeks. I think he had left our
world, to wander in a world between this one and
the Other. His body seemed thirsty for the juices
and potions I prepared for him to drink. But he
was unaware of his state, unable to eat, speechless
and deaf, his eyes always closed. Never before

had I seen a man so tormented by loving. I
sometimes wept after leaving his cell.

☼

About a month after he was brought to
Tintagel, Lancelot returned to this world. Elis,
one of the squires charged with his care, ran to
tell me that Lancelot had awakened and was
raging in his cell like a wild animal, wildly shouting strange noises, tearing his shirt and bedding
cloths.

I ordered Alun, the other squire, to go to
Lancelot's cell to help Elis. I watched Lancelot
beat and throw the two squires like toys in his
mad fury. It was utterly impossible for those two
strong young men to subdue him.

I knew that sooner or later Lancelot would
exhaust himself, so I told the battered squires to
withdraw and lock the cell door. His screeching
followed us as we walked out of the secret corridor.

Next day Lancelot's howlings ceased. I
ordered the squires to bring a midday dish of
meats and vegetables to him. He ate ravenously,
threw the dish at the squires when they came to
retrieve it, and slammed the door shut as they left
the cell. Then he was quiet for almost a week
thereafter. Every day the squires brought him the

midday meal, set it on the floor of his cell, and then swiftly closed and locked his door.

☆

At the end of a week of relative calm, Elis and Alun came running to me to tell me that Lancelot had escaped from his cell when they opened the door to set down his dish. He had waited for the noise of their arrival and had flung the door open, knocking them off their feet as he threw himself out of the cell. He ran down the corridor and out of the hospital, but they were unable to catch him. Then they asked me to come with them to see what he had drawn on the walls of his cell.

He may have used a pointed chicken or lamb bone to draw the scenes of men and women in the great hall at Cadbury Castle, and some pictures of a man and a woman in a bedchamber. All the lines were red. So Lancelot must have pricked himself to make the drawings with his own blood.

After a quick glance at the drawings I ordered the squires to lock the cell door and to forbid entry to anyone. Then I went back to my own bedchamber.

I tried to fall asleep. But I could not escape from the stirring images that Lancelot's drawings had burned into my mind. I left my bed, took up a torch and went to the hospital corridor. Tintagel was asleep. No one had seen me. I unlocked the door and entered Lancelot's cell. I remember the faint smell of his sweat in the room.

I sat on the edge of Lancelot's bed. He had made pictures of his secret devotion to Guinevere. Guinevere wore her crown, and Lancelot had drawn his own face in profile. The anguish in their faces flooded each picture.

I moved closer to the wall to study them in the flickering light. Guinevere and Lancelot were drawn as I had made my tapestry figures when I was a girl, stick bodies with clear heads and faces. Each scene, no larger than than the palm of my hand, was framed by a square outline.

Arthur, Guinevere, and Merlin seated at the midday meal in Cadbury's great hall. Guinevere, her eyes downcast, alone. The two lovers gazing into each other's eyes, their lips downturned in sadness. Guinevere, alone, looking to Lancelot approaching her bed. Guinevere extending her arms to embrace him. The lovers entwined under the sheepskin cover, only their faces visible. Lancelot kneeling in prayer beside the bed as Guinevere gazes at him.

How deeply bewildered and helpless they were. I turned away from the wall and told myself that I must not weep.

I could imagine their desperate awareness of the traps their god had set for them. Guinevere would now be suffering as I did, after that magical time when I loved Accolon. Perhaps such longing for another can be felt only once in the course of one's life. But whatever may have remained of my old wish for revenge against Guinevere was washed away by what I saw in those drawings. Guinevere and Lancelot were lost in a whirlpool of enchantment, far deeper than my own with Guiomar.

I realized that I must continue to protect Lancelot even in his absence. So I filled a large dish with water, took some cloths and washed away Lancelot's drawings. While I rinsed and soaked the cloths I saw the water darken, like iron mould, with his blood.

I remember that when I returned to my bedchamber I asked my gods and goddesses to protect the three lovers, Guinevere, Arthur, and Lancelot. I remained awake in my bed until the red glow of the rising sun flooded the window slit. Then I fell into a deep sleep, without dreaming.

☼

I began to hear rumors from visitors to Tintagel about fantastic happenings at my hospital and inn. I believe that Merlin, having learned that I had cared for Lancelot at Tintagel, might have devised such rumors to conceal his own subtle schemes. He would have preferred Lancelot's death, to remove him forever from the possibility of smirching Arthur's prestige. And adultery committed by a Christian queen was punishable by death at the stake.

Morgause came to visit me at Tintagel and told me of the turmoil and chatter among the ladies at Cadbury. She said that Arthur had refused to believe the charges against Guinevere and Lancelot, despite the exposure of their "sin." She went on to tell of the bishop's feverish efforts to resolve the issue, and that the Roman pope had insisted that Arthur must neither reject Guinevere nor punish her. And that Lodegrance, Guinevere's father, who had become a Christian long before Arthur had become king, may have pleaded with the bishop for mercy for his daughter.

My own status in the reigning family was called into question. They proposed that I had conspired to protect Lancelot from punishment. Morgause said that she believed that Merlin was quietly insinuating that I was using my knowledge of potions to transform some of the men and women who came to Tintagel into monsters of greed, lasciviousness, and blind violence. I was called a sorceress, evil, even though I had transformed the castle at Tintagel into a place for healing and refuge.

Morgause then told me that Niniane, the vivid, beautiful young woman whom I had taken as my helper to Gorlot years before, had won Merlin's utter devotion. He moved into a helpless enchantment whenever she came into his presence.

I, in turn, had become Merlin's scapegoat.

✿

I come to the end of my telling now, without tears, for my eyes have no more to shed. There are times when my sorrow pierces deep within my body. But I have at last learned from my gods and goddesses how to carry that sorrow, those wounds, in silence.

Dear Ceinwen!

✿

Arthur had somehow learned of the drawings that Lancelot had made on the wall of his cell at Tintagel. Could one of my squires have said something while besotted? It doesn't matter now.

To preserve his honor in the fellowship of Christian knights, Arthur decided to defy the order from Rome. He charged Guinevere as an adulteress and ordered that she be burned at the stake. And he declared his resolve to kill Lancelot for his betrayal.

I have imagined Arthur's anguish over those decisions. I knew that, in his callow fashion, he loved Guinevere. And I could imagine how complex was the web the three had spun together, for Arthur had admired and cherished Lancelot as a warrior, and as a model for the other knights.

Merlin and the bishop urged Arthur to punish Lancelot alone, but Arthur was unmovable. Somehow Lancelot learned at the last moment of Arthur's intention to execute Guinevere.

She was tied to a stake in the courtyard and the torch was about to set the pyre aflame when Lancelot ripped into the crowd with five of his French warriors. He cut the ropes that bound Guinevere while his warriors fought off Arthur's men. With Guinevere seated behind him on his splendid horse, Lancelot slashed at Gaheris, Morgause's youngest son, killing him instantly, and raced away. Utterly unprepared for the ferocity of Lancelot's raid, Arthur's men could not prevent their escape.

☼

Sir Gawain, Gaheris's oldest brother, raged at Arthur to avenge Gaheris's death. Arthur mustered a force of his lords and warriors to cross the channel, to lay siege to Lancelot's castle in Brittany. Guinevere persuaded Lancelot to allow her to return to Cadbury, because she feared the outcome if she remained with him. Lancelot, in torment, agreed.

Before Arthur set sail for Brittany he ordered Mordred to serve as his regent during his absence from Cadbury. At the same time that Arthur began the siege against Lancelot's castle at Benoic, Guinevere sailed to Britain and returned to Cadbury.

At Cadbury, Mordred made no secret of his lust for Guinevere, and forced her to enjoy him. He then rashly declared himself the new ruler of the Britons, and Guinevere his queen. Guinevere despised him, and sent word to Arthur about Mordred's betrayal. Arthur immediately ended his siege against Lancelot's castle, returned to Britain with his warriors, and declared war on Mordred.

Mordred arrogantly accepted Arthur's challenge. So the small force of Cadbury warriors would fight against their own comrades, at Camlann.

✿

To escape punishment for his part in the deception involving Excalibur, in the duel between

Arthur and Accolon, Erec had ridden off from Cadbury to a distant village, where he was unknown. He grew a beard to disguise himself, and found a home and work on a small farm with an old, lonely farmer who treated him kindly. Then Erec was conscripted into Arthur's army when Arthur set out to besiege Lancelot. But he was able to conceal his true identity.

In the battle against Mordred at Camlann, Erec received a severe hip wound, and he was one of the injured warriors who came from Camlann to my hospital at Tintagel. I assumed the responsibility for his treatment, and we were able to talk easily while he was recovering.

☼

Arthur and Mordred's forces faced each other on a broad green meadow at Camlann, where Arthur's warriors had encamped on their journey back to Cadbury. The bloody slaughter, in that battle between the two groups of the finest warriors in Britain, drenched the meadow as red as a field of poppies. All the knights of the Round Table met their deaths at Camlann. Only a small number of foot soldiers survived.

The custom of honor in warfare demanded that the leaders of opposing forces must fight each other. So Arthur, my half-brother, and Mordred, his son and mine, stood face to face, ignorant of their kinship, to draw each other's blood in their fight to the death. In a circle made by some wounded, exhausted warriors, Arthur and Mordred stood and thrust and chopped at each other. While Erec lustily described their sword play I wept, thinking of the shame and the rage, the gigantic ambitions and failures that had fed those murderous energies.

Mordred slowly dropped to his knees, bleeding from Excalibur's slashes, while he desperately parried Arthur's butchery. Arthur, severely wounded and sagging, raised Excalibur to chop at Mordred again. As he was about to give my son the death blow, Arthur slowly collapsed across Mordred's body and was stabbed in his gut by Mordred's upthrust sword.

Mordred's body was left on the battlefield. Arthur was placed in a wagon that carried him to die at my hospital. In my mind's eye I saw poor Mordred's scarlet birthmark, bathed in his and his father's blood.

✧

Ceinwen, those deaths are now in the slowly dimming past. Shouldn't I bring my telling to this very moment? You and I in this room, warmed by your lovely tapestries? Niniane and Ettarde at work in the hospital rooms?

My life did not end with the deaths of Mordred, my son, and Arthur, his father, my brother. My sorrows for those two fated men are stones I shall carry in my heart into the Otherworld.

So to complete this tapestry I shall continue my telling to include Niniane and Ettarde, so different from each other, yet so necessary to my hospital and inn.

✩

Ettarde came to my hospital two years ago, exhausted, mumbling wild, unconnected words. She looked like one of our old village hags. When we undressed her to wash her matted hair and filthy body we found a tight copper chain around her belly, green with her sweat. Why does she wear such a harsh cinch? Who made it for her? Was she kept on a leash?

We did not remove the chain and she wears it even now. We have tried to nourish her wasted body and damaged spirit. But all we can make out of her mumblings are a raging disgust for her father and her "hateful two brothers and all other men." She sometimes mumbles "Sir Gawain," so she must have known him. When we ask her to tell us about him, she twists her face and makes ugly sounds from deep in her throat.

After some weeks in the hospital we told her that we had done all we could to restore her to health. We would have urged her to leave the hospital to find her home again, but we were afraid that she could come to harm, traveling without an escort in her bewildered state. So we offered her the safety of Tintagel if she would agree to help us in the hospital.

When she understood what we were asking her to do, she fell to her knees and begged us to allow her to stay with us.

We taught her how to bathe the girls and women who came to the hospital with their ailments. At first she suddenly stopped whatever she was doing to mutter curses against all men, in the vilest language I have ever heard. But we have been able to persuade her not to do that in the presence of the women, by threatening to remove her from work in the hospital.

The only man she was permitted to attend was Arthur as he lay waiting for his death. I had ordered continuous nursing for him, day and night, and Ettarde was given the work of washing him. She had learned to bathe her patients deftly and gently, so Niniane and I told her to clean Arthur's terrible wounds. She wept helplessly when she first saw his butchered body. For the first time in our experience with her she did not mutter those curses.

Arthur's passage saddened us, but we knew that we had done all that could be done for him. Not even Merlin could have restored that butchered body to health again. Ettarde kept to her room for a week after we saw Arthur's boat take him across the water to the Otherworld. I do not think that we shall ever learn what caused her festering hatred of men.

☼

And Niniane, yes, Niniane.

Where to begin? I have told how I met her at my wedding to Uryens, singing so beautifully at the feast. And how she came to Gorlot with me, how she learned to make potions in my workroom there, and how she resisted my wish to become her friend. How I grew disaffected by her nagging at me to teach her the secrets of Merlin's dark magic. And how I sent her back to Cadbury Castle.

Niniane came to Tintagel a few weeks after Lancelot's escape from the hospital. She asked if I would take her into service.

I remembered that Morgause had told me about the rumors of Merlin's enchantment with her. So at first I thought that Merlin had sent her to spy on me. I bluntly asked whether that was indeed her purpose.

She replied bitterly, "Lady Morgain, do not fear. I hate him. I hate Merlin, and shall hate him forever. But he will not believe me, and he seeks to enjoy me whenever he comes near me. He is mad."

I pressed Niniane to tell me why she resisted him. She was silent for a few moments, twisting her lips. Then she said that she had sworn to obey her father's dying wish that she never be ensnared by enjoyment with any man, and that she never marry.

I am still unsure whether that was the truth, or whether she invented the vow to conceal her fear of men. Or to conceal her disgust with their bodies?

But I no longer tolerate resistance to my questions. Niniane and I are well past the time of maidens' games, so I insisted I must know whether she was telling the truth. Had she really made such a vow?

I saw her face grow sombre, her lips downturning in what seemed to be sorrow, or self-pity. She silently, slowly nodded, "Yes."

I accepted her expression of sorrow, if it was that. I have indeed known enjoyment, and how it cleansed and refreshed my body and mind.

And I have also kept my vow to remain chaste after Accolon's death.

Niniane went on to say that Merlin refused to believe her protests, that every day, beginning on the first day she began to work in the medicine room at Cadbury Castle, Merlin would beseech her, and that he had clawed at her clothing as if he was besotted.

One night, after Merlin behaved that way in the presence of some men of the court, Niniane decided to leave Cadbury and seek service at Tintagel.

While she was at Gorlot, Niniane never spoke of her vow to remain virgin. I knew that she was approached by one or another of Uryens's young knights. But I also know that she did not permit any intimacy. Accolon would have known, and would have told me.

Niniane is no longer the simple, obsessed maiden. She is still beautiful, with her green, flashing eyes and dark blonde hair. She is well past the age for childbearing. But her gaze, like her luxurious body, seems heavy with the wish for enjoyment. I believe there is a secret center in Niniane that enables her to use other people without shame.

I can see how Merlin's resistance to loving might have been dissolved by such a woman. And

I know too that Niniane must be aware of the wish for enjoyment that she can stimulate in men, because I knew that power in myself before I took my vow. It is a weapon, a knife that all women can learn to use. So she may have used that weapon on Merlin.

I know how sharp that knife can be.

Niniane is skillful in the making of the potions and salves we use in the hospital, and so has relieved me from much of that work. She has not spoken of her old wish to learn Merlin's magic potions, but she may have learned some of them from him. I am certain that one of Niniane's own medicines helped to give Arthur a few more hours of painless life.

I remember how, when Arthur was brought to my hospital in that hopelessly butchered body, Niniane's anguish brought her to tears that she swiftly calmed by her will.

Could she have felt love for Arthur? I saw a tenderness in her manner toward him that I never saw in any other circumstances. I could see that she touched him with love in her fingertips. Of course she would never have had the occasion to reveal that love to him because she was, after all, a village woman, not of noble birth.

As I say that, I think I can understand Merlin's obsession and enchantment. It was so unlike the Merlin I once knew. He would never have beseeched a noblewoman in the presence of others. I well remember how secretive he was about our enjoyments. And I think Niniane may have played on Merlin's imprisoned lust. The very difference in their stations would have goaded Merlin's desire.

So I can imagine Merlin's wrenching pain now, when he cannot have even the simple pleasure of looking at the woman who enchants him so deeply.

☼

A few days after our mourning for Arthur had ended, Niniane and I sat together at supper. She seemed calmer and somewhat more at ease with me. It was a sweet, warm evening in late spring, so I invited her to come with me to sit on one of the lower parapets. We wrapped ourselves in the sheepskins I kept there. I had spent many evenings alone up there, thinking and remembering, watching the wonderful slow circling of the night sky around the North Star.

I remembered Niniane's hands as she tended Arthur's wounds, and the swift wisp of the thought that she may have loved him. Because she was Merlin's handmaiden at Cadbury, she might have observed the behavior of Arthur, Guinevere, and Lancelot, the three whose secrets would bring about the destruction of the Round Table and the dream of a new Britain.

We silently watched the great display in the darkening sky. Then I surprised her by asking whether she had been present when Lancelot arrived to join the Round Table.

I knew that my question startled her, exactly as I intended it. She turned to me with a question in her eyes. She had always been quick to evade my probing. So I repeated my question. After a few moments she said, "Yes. Everyone was present. Everyone had been told of his prowess, and everyone was eager to see him at last. Some of the older knights didn't look with pleasure to his arrival."

I had to press Niniane to tell all that I wanted to know. She would speak only in answer to my questions, and then she would become silent. But I persisted.

Immediately after his arrival at Cadbury, Lancelot was called by Arthur to demonstrate his skill at arms in a bout with Gawain, Morgause's eldest son. Sticks served as swords. If real weapons had been used instead, Gawain would have lost his life on that day.

Lancelot was superior in all the tests of swordsmanship, archery, and fighting on horseback. It was immediately clear that no other knight had ever proved himself so dangerous a warrior. Niniane, like me, detested warriors' murderous skills. So she turned her attention to Arthur and Guinevere as they watched the two men fight.

Arthur sat quietly, keenly studying Lancelot's maneuvers to grasp the secrets underlying his unusual prowess.

But Guinevere's cool, pale face began to flush with what Niniane suspected was pleasure, the thrilling pleasure of watching an extraordinary man moving at first so like a quiet brook, then a swift river, and finlly a crushing, inescapable torrent. Merlin, sitting next to Niniane, voiced little grunts of appreciation. In those brief moments Lancelot had captured everyone's admiration by the images he drew with his lean, powerful body and mind.

When those bouts ended Arthur and Guinevere arose to express their pleasure at Lancelot's entry into the Round Table. Niniane saw Gawain's ill-concealed dismay. Niniane said that Gawain had always appeared to be proud, even vain, about his position among the knights of the Round Table. Now he knew he would be displaced from his high station as the chief defender of his king and queen.

Poor Gawain, dead at Camlann, defending Arthur's honor.

☼

When Lancelot turned to receive Guinevere's praise Niniane noticed Guinevere's blushing face and her oddly halting words. Niniane trembled as she watched Lancelot silently looking up to Guinevere, already deep in enchantment. Niniane said that she had never talked about that memory with anyone before our conversation that night on the parapet.

I knew this was an opportunity for me to learn more, because Niniane's recounting of what she had seen and remembered was so acute. So, under the peaceful stars, I continued to press my questions. She realized that I was not to be deterred, and she softened to tell me what little she knew about the tormented love between Guinevere and Lancelot.

Within a few months after Lancelot's arrival, rumors of their secret enjoyments began to be whispered in the court. I asked Niniane if she had suspected Guinevere and Lancelot of committing what the bishop would call a "sin." She said that she was never in a situation that would enable her to know that.

But she described the uproar at Cadbury after the four lords had broken into Guinevere's room. The wives of the Cadbury lords felt, or pretended to feel, disgraced by Guinevere's fall from honor. The men exchanged their imagined, crude details of the lovers' enjoyments. But they were not disturbed by the death of young Lord Aliers.

And Merlin? Had he foreseen the devastation that Lancelot would bring to Arthur's kingship and his dreams for the future of Britain?

Had Merlin foreseen Lancelot's devastating force?

Or was he too tired, or too sick with desire for Niniane, to care any longer about the future of Britain?

Niniane remains closed, uninterested in friendship with me, or with any other person for that matter. And I have no need for friendship with her. She is a fine nurse.

☼

You, dear Ceinwen, are all I need. Will you renounce your vow of silence now?

You press your lips together and shake your head, "No."

Well then, Ceinwen, I have ended my telling.

But there is something more that I wish you to write.

Yes?

Do you remember the song we made and sang so often, before you took your vow? You must write it down as I sing it to you, so we can join our words in the wonderful compact we made so many years ago. Write, Ceinwen!

When all is said and done,
When all is dust and bone,
What will earth remember?
The fine-toothed comb of mind
watching its coils unwind?
And what will air remember?
The murmur of one voice
urging the other's choice?
And what will water remember?
The tipping caress of my bosom's pair
in the cool, sweet wetness of your hair?
And fire, what will fire remember?
How fire did rage and ignite the moans
of love's denial of dust and bone?

✿ ✿ ✿